WHAT IF?

A book of the some of the greatest ever transfer rumours and what would have happened had they gone through

R.M. Skillen

Raider Publishing International

New York   London   Cape Town

Published By Raider Publishing International
www.RaiderPublishing.com
New York London Cape Town
Printed in the United States of America and the United Kingdom

Dedicated to Renata, Neve and Anakin, who have put up with me talking about nothing but this book for the last nine months. Thank you. I could never have done it without your love and support.

WHAT IF?

A book of the some of the greatest ever transfer rumours and what would have happened had they gone through

---

R.M. Skillen

Introduction

THEY SAY THAT MONEY MAKES THE WORLD GO AROUND. Well, never is this truer than in the football world. The back pages of newspapers are constantly jam packed with stories of the latest transfers. Who is going where, and for how much sometimes becomes more entertaining than football itself, especially if you're a Blackburn Rovers fan.

I love the transfer rumour mill so much that I even clocked up a hefty telephone bill calling the Liverpool Club call line that told me we were signing everyone from Zinedine Zidane to a fictional player from TV's, Dream Team show. But that is just it. Most of what we read and hear is utter bullshit. As soon as we hear it we know it is crap, a rumour told to sell papers, put forward by an agent to try and secure their client the move of their dreams, or to dupe a 13 year old kid into calling a premium rate phone number.

Despite knowing that Zidane would never have been seen dead in a Liverpool shirt, it never stopped my excitement brewing and exploding with the thought of the mercurial Frenchman lifting the Premiership trophy at Anfield. It is an excitement that, I am sure, grips every fan of the beautiful game, all over the world, at some point in time.

At the end of the day we love the gossip. It fuels our passion for the clubs we love and our dreams about the success that could come our way if we would just sign that certain player. With that in mind, here are the stories behind some of the greatest ever transfer rumours, and what would have happened to the players and clubs involved had they come true. Remember small decisions can make or break careers.

Is Pele the Best Ever

PELE IS CONSIDERED BY MANY AS THE GREATEST PLAYER to ever pull on a pair of boots and kick some inflated pig skin around a field. He scored an amazing 1087 goals over his 20 year career that also included three World Cup winners' medals. But despite all his obvious successes there are still those that feel he cannot be recognized as the greatest player to ever walk the planet because he never proved himself on the glitz and glamour stage of Europe.

"I played in European football for 10 years while Pele played in South America. Yes, he won World Cups and everything, but playing in Europe is something else entirely. When I played, the man-markers in Spanish and Italian football were like hunting dogs. They never left me alone. When people voted to determine the best player ever in 2000, he came second, behind me. And there was another vote in Brazil in which he came second, behind Ayrton Senna. He needs to stop coming second," said Argentinean superstar Diego Maradona in an interview with *FIFA.com.*

It wasn't that he never had the offers to move abroad. In fact, he almost moved abroad on several occasions. Manchester United were once thought have made a bid for him, but it was Italian club Juventus, and Spanish mega club, Real Madrid, that came the closest to securing his signature.

In 1975 Pele shocked the football world when he signed

for North American Soccer League club (NASL) the New York Cosmos. America was seen by many within the game as the last frontier for football, where it fell well behind the likes of baseball, basketball and American football in terms of popularity. In 1974 The New York Cosmos averaged less than 4,000 spectators at home games. But that was before the great Pele signed for the club.

Pele had been in semi retirement since 1972, but had considered taking up an offer from Real Madrid to start playing again on a full time basis. The move would have given him the opportunity to play alongside the likes of Antonio Camacho and Juan Roberto Martínez, as well as the chance to conquer European football and cement his status as the ultimate legend of the game. But Pele decided against the move to Spain, preferring to run down his final years of playing football in the USA for the New York Cosmos. The move still baffles many within the game. Why would anyone turn down the chance to play in front of 80,000 passionate fans at the Estadio Santiago Bernabéu? There are a couple of theories as to what was going through his mind when he put pen to paper on a three year Cosmos deal. The first is that it was purely a case of money. The Cosmos were owned by the Warner Communications Company which had a cheque book to rival any in Europe. In an attempt to lift the profile of the game in America and increase their measly attendances they left that cheque book wide open with Pele being the first big name to arrive. The plan seemed to have worked, and by 1979 46,000 people were watching the Cosmos play every week. But after the owners began to tighten the purse strings in an attempt to balance the books, the big names began to leave along with the supporters, and in 1984 the club went bankrupt. Other clubs soon followed suit, causing the total collapse of the league. It was a dramatic downfall, and caused the football hierarchy in America to rethink the total structure of the game.

While money could have played a big part in Pele's decision, many feel that there was no reason that he couldn't be earning a similar amount in Spain, and that the move to America was made purely to buff up the big man's ego. He was used to being the superstar at Brazilian club Santos and within the Brazilian national squad. If he had signed for Real Madrid he would have been just another player vying for a spot in an already star studded line up, and that would have done nothing for the Pele brand name. In America, he would once again be the legend, the superstar, the untouchable one, with everyone licking his arse just the way he liked it. It is a theory that seems to be backed up by his reluctance to leave Santos when he was at the peak of his powers. With a string of high profile European clubs fighting it out for his signature, a deal was apparently lined up that would take him to Juventus, with Italian car manufacturer Fiat stumping a lot of the cash needed to help the move go ahead. But Pele declined, preferring to remain in the relative safety of his home country with the club where he was simply known as "The King".

Real Madrid wanted me, along with Manchester United, and Juventus. In fact, the Juventus president almost reached a deal with Santos which included support from Fiat. I thought about coming to Europe a lot, but I preferred to stay with the team in my heart, Santos.
PELE ON WHY HE NEVER MOVED TO EUROPE.

What If?

ITALIAN CLUB JUVENTUS COMPLETED THE SIGNING of Brazilian superstar, Pele, on 1st September 1968. A staggering world record fee of 2 million GBP was paid, smashing the previous record of 500,000 GBP that was also paid by Juventus for Pietro Anastasi.

The historical transfer was mostly funded by Italian car manufacturer Fiat who disregarded criticism that was thrown at them for wearing their football colours on their sleeve by saying, "The move will bring Italian football to the forefront of the world and help every club attract better players because they will all want to face the great Pele."

It was hard to disagree with the statement after every major newspaper in the world had the story of the two time world cup winner's transfer emblazoned across their front page. Suddenly Pele and Juventus were all anybody wanted to talk about, and when the new king of Italy lined up for his first training session, the Juventus board were forced to hold it at their home ground, The Stadio Olimpico di Torino. The stadium was half filled by the world's press, while the remaining seats were sold off to the highest bidders. The atmosphere was more like a European Cup final than a mundane training session, as everyone inside expected to see something amazing take place.

Forty five minutes passed with some simple stretching exercises and ball drills being the only action. Every now and then, Pele would wave to the crowd or do some keepie uppies just to make sure the press had something to print for the next morning's back pages. But just as the stadium was beginning to empty, and the five aside session was winding down, Pele went on something of a mazy run, side stepping one challenge before sticking the ball through the legs of another. He was about to tap the ball into the empty net when midfielder, Adolfo Gori, hunted him down like a dog and came in from the side with a crunching challenge. The stadium lit up with camera flashes as each and every photographer in the ground tried their best to get the perfect shot of the world's most expensive player rolling around in agony on the floor.

It was a total disaster for Juventus, and Pele, who had totally destroyed his right knee. The medical staff thought that he would miss at least a year, but if they were being honest even that was optimistic. After several operations and several failed comebacks, Pele finally retired from the sport just days before the 1970 World Cup was due to begin. It was a sad end to a career that had promised so much.

The Italian press were devastated by the news of Pele's long term injury and labelled Gori as "The King Killer," demanding that he be sold abroad and banned from playing in Italy ever again. But in January 1969 he was simply sacked by Juventus and never played football again.

In a 2002 interview with *Four Four Two magazine* Gori showed no remorse for the tackle that prematurely ended the career of one of the greatest ever players, saying, "It was simply my way of saying 'Welcome to Italy'. If he couldn't handle me marking him there was no way he would have survived playing in Europe."

A World Cup Winner in Sheffield

DIEGO ARMANDO MARADONA IS, QUITE SIMPLY, the greatest football talent the world has ever seen. Say what you will about the man's off field exploits, when he pulled on his boots there was no disputing his genius. At 5ft 5 inches, Maradona was not only short, but his stocky build gave him a low centre of gravity that allowed him to twist, turn and escape defenders with relative ease. Add to that a chess player's brain that was always ten steps ahead of everybody else, a good turn of pace, a great left foot, a good right foot, an eye for goal and unbelievable ability to pick out passes and you can see why many rate Maradona as the best of the best.

An Argentinos Juniors scout by the name of Francis Cornejo discovered Diego Maradona playing football with his friends on a waste ground near his home in Lanus, a poor suburb of Buenos Aires. Although he was he was only ten years old, Cornejo instantly recognized the young Maradona as a special talent and took him under his wing.

Before Cornejo died at the age of 76 he described his role in Maradona's career by saying that he was "happy for having painted one of the most beautiful paintings of all."

Maradona was soon a key part of the Argentinos Juniors youth team known as, *Los Cebollitas,* or The Little

Onions, as they went unbeaten for 136 games. At just 12 years old he was already becoming something of a local legend at Argentinos, entertaining the supporters at home games by doing seemingly impossible keepie ups. His rise through the youth ranks was quick, and impressive, and he made his first team debut on 20 October 1976 at just 15.

A year later, and the buzz surrounding the precocious young talent was phenomenal. The Argentine public was screaming for him to be included in the World Cup squad and clubs all over Europe were lining up to secure his signature. Talks of a move to Barcelona, Real Madrid or Roma were rife, but for some strange reason it was English second division side, Sheffield Utd, that came the closest to stealing him away from his home country.

It was during a scouting mission to South America when Utd coach, Harry Haslam, desperate to add some flair to his struggling team, approached Argentinos Juniors about signing the young Diego Maradona. Haslam was known for his persuasiveness in the transfer market and after some negotiations he managed to set up a deal that would bring the hottest young talent in the world to Bramall Lane. There are many different theories about what the actual fee agreed upon was. Some say that it was a measly 200,000 GBP. Others say that Haslam managed to talk Argentinos down from 1 million GBP to just 600,000 GBP. But whatever the amount, it was apparently too much for the Sheffield Utd board, and they told Haslam to find a cheaper alternative. Utd ended up signing Alex Sabela from River Plate for 150,000 GBP instead. Sabela did become a bit of a cult figure to the Sheffield Utd fans scoring eight goals in 76 games and exciting them with his free flowing style of play. But in 1980, just two years after they signed Sabela, the Sheffield Utd board cashed in and sold him to Leeds Utd for 400,000 GBP. All the while, the rise of Maradona continued, and in 1982 he became the world's most expensive player when he joined Barcelona from Boca Juniors for a whopping 5 million GBP, leaving all at Sheffield Utd wondering what could have been.

What If?

A 17 YEAR OLD WIDE EYED, BUSHY HAIRED KID BY the name of Diego Armando Maradona pulled on the red and white striped shirt of Sheffield Utd for the first time against Mansfield on the 4th March 1978. Maradona announced his arrival in England in style. He pinged passes all over the pitch with ease, ran at defenders with pace and skill and early in the second half scored an overhead kick that is still talked about on the terraces at Bramall Lane as one of the greatest goals ever scored. But this new found confidence in The Blades was short lived and after seven goals in four dazzling displays, Liverpool Manager Bob Paisley made it his goal to sign this amazing youngster.

"I watched the game against Mansfield and was dumb struck by this little kid doing seemingly impossible things with the ball. I just had to have him at Anfield," said Paisley in a 1981 interview with *The Liverpool Echo*.

In a move that shocked the football world, Diego Maradona put pen to paper on a five year Liverpool deal for around 2.5 million GBP on 20th March 1978. The fee was seen to be crazy by many in the business at the time, but it proved to be money well spent as Maradona went on to become the club's greatest ever goal scorer with 402 goals over 15 years, as he guided them to seven European titles, five FA Cups and 11 English League titles as well as 4 World Club Championships. He won the FIFA world player of the year award a record 5 times and was quite simply the greatest footballing talent we have ever seen.

The 1986 World Cup

IT HAPPENED DURING LIVERPOOL'S 4-0 THUMPING of local rivals Everton in the 1986 FA Cup final. The job of marking Maradona had gone to Everton and England midfielder Peter Reid, but it was pretty safe to say that Reid had come off second best. Maradona had already scored one and played a major part in the other three, when he found himself in acres of space wide on the right with just 10 minutes of the match remaining. Reid looked tired as he traipsed after the Argentinean on the large Wembley pitch. As he tried to close him down, Maradona produced another of his trade mark step overs and left Reid face first in the dirt. Maradona put on the accelerator and charged toward the Everton goal with the ball seemingly glued to his feet. The Liverpool fans were expectant as he set to let fly with another left foot shot. But Maradona pulled up suddenly, holding his left thigh. Liverpool manager Kenny Dalglish quickly pulled his star player from the field, but with the World Cup in Mexico just a few short weeks away the whole of Argentina held their breath hoping that their Captain would make it to the first game.

The prognosis from the Liverpool doctors wasn't good. Maradona had suffered a slight hamstring strain and it was recommended that he miss the first few games in Mexico. But Maradona was a proud man and he didn't want to let his country down. Although he was only half fit he lined up

in Argentina's first group game against the Korean
Republic. Argentina won 3-1 and Maradona went on to
dominate the group stages scoring an important goal in the
1-1 draw with Italy, guiding his side to top spot in Group
A. Argentina progressed to the quarter final stage after a 1-0
victory over Uruguay to set up a clash with Maradona's
adopted country, England.

The two sides were evenly matched early on, but it
didn't take long for Diego to take control, and the English
were lucky to survive without conceding until halftime.
Five minutes into the second half and Maradona was
chasing a long ball played in behind the England defence. It
looked like the little Argentinean had no chance of reaching
it, but after a little burst of speed he found himself
challenging England goalkeeper Peter Shilton for the ball. As
the 5ft 5 inch Maradona tried to out jump the 6ft tall
keeper, his standing leg seemed to give way and he
screamed in agony, clattering into Shilton, leaving them both
spread eagled on the edge of the box. The ball had evaded
them both and trickled into the back of the net and the
Argentina fans all over the world started to celebrate. But
referee, Ali Bin Nasser, had already blown his whistle
signalling for an England free kick and the goal was ruled
out. To make matters worse Maradona was stretchered
from the field with what was later said to be a torn
hamstring. He would miss the first two months of the new
season with Liverpool, but, more importantly, his
dominating presence was gone from the Argentina side.

Just three minutes later, England forward Peter
Beardsley picked up the ball on the halfway line. The
crowd seemed to sense that something special was coming
and all 115,000 people inside the Estadio Azteca seemed to
stand and gasp in anticipation. Even the Argentina fans
were amazed and applauded as Beardsley went on a mazy
run, ghosting past Oscar Ruggeri. He carved through the

Argentina defence as if they weren't there, beating Jose Lewis Brown with a little drop of the shoulder before rounding goalkeeper, Nery Pumpido, and sliding the ball into the back of the empty net. The goal not only gave England a vital lead but it also went down as one of the greatest goals in football history, and in 2001 Beardsley was knighted by the Queen for his efforts.

Gary Lineker went on to seal a 2-0 victory for England who eventually went on to lift the trophy by beating West Germany 1-0 in the final, after Lineker scored something of a controversial goal. England winger John Barnes whipped in a cross, and as Lineker dived to head the ball it seemed to bounce off his right arm and trickle into the goal. Asked after the game whether he had handled the ball on purpose, Lineker replied, "God was guiding everything I did." The press from all over the world were quick to comment, and labelled the goal as coming from the hand of god.

IF ONLY THE WORLD WERE PERFECT.

Ferguson the Gooner

THE NAME OF ALEX FERGUSON IS SYNONYMOUS WITH just one club, Manchester Utd. Since he took over on the 6th of November 1986 Manchester Utd have become the dominant force in English football. By the end of the 2008-2009 season they had won the English Premier League a staggering 11 times, and the European Champions League twice, with Alex Ferguson becoming known by many as the greatest coach the world has ever seen. His ability to build sides with a mixture of experience and youth that play with attacking flair and imagination is definitely second to none. But it was an ability already evident in his first managerial position at lowly Scottish side East Stirlingshire, while he was earning just 40 GBP per week. While there, he also became known as a strong disciplinarian, with former player Bobby McCulley describing him as a "terrifying bastard." But it was his tactical knowledge that won over his players and, at the age of 32 he was already on the verge of greatness.

He only lasted at East Stirlingshire for one year before he was poached by St. Mirren. Even though St. Mirren was lower in the league it was seen as a bigger club and the decision to move was an easy one. In 1977 it appeared Ferguson had worked his magic as St Mirren won the second division title. Surprisingly, though, just one year later, Ferguson was sacked for the first and last time in his career. There are many different theories as to why St. Mirren remains the only club to have wielded the axe to the great one. But at the trial put forward by Ferguson for unfair dismissal he was described as "petty and immature" with "no managerial ability" by the St. Mirren Chairman, Willie Todd. In 2008 Todd did an interview with *The Guardian* in which he said that Ferguson's dismissal was down to a simple breach of contract. Apparently, Ferguson had agreed to take over at Aberdeen without telling his current employers and was already trying to poach players and staff.

Ferguson took over at Aberdeen in June 1978 and in 1980 they won the Scottish first division, becoming the first club other that Celtic or Rangers to win the trophy since Kilmarnock in 1965. Ferguson's success didn't end there and he would lift the trophy twice more, in 1984 and '85 as well as guiding his side to a 2-1 victory over Spanish giants, Real Madrid in the Cup Winners' Cup final on the 11th of May 1983.

Big clubs from south of the border were now starting to take notice, with Tottenham Hotspur, Arsenal and Manchester Utd leading the chase. In 1985 Ferguson briefly took charge of the Scotland squad after the sudden death of manager Jock Stein. He agreed to take his country through to the 1986 World Cup finals in Mexico and no further as he hoped a move to England would soon follow. Just before the Scotland squad set out for the World Cup Finals, Ferguson apparently had talks with Arsenal and a tentative agreement between the two parties was agreed upon. Arsenal were desperate to make sure that no other club would come along with a better offer and they urged Ferguson to make the move official before the Scotland squad set out for Mexico, but Ferguson refused.

Former Scotland goal keeper, Jim Leighton, remembers the situation, "Ferguson was offered the Arsenal job," said

Leighton. "George Graham would have been his assistant, but he wanted to wait until the World Cup was finished before it was announced. Arsenal said they wanted it [a decision] straight away and so he refused it, and George Graham got the job. Alex wanted to announce it when he got back to Aberdeen. He wanted to do it the right way."

Alex Ferguson eventually took over at Manchester Utd in November 1986 and the rest, as they say, is history.

What If?

AFTER SCOTLAND FINISHED BOTTOM OF GROUP E WITH just one point at the 1986 World Cup in Mexico, Alex Ferguson decided enough was enough and he stepped down as Manager. Despite Scotland's relatively poor performance, Ferguson still found himself to be something of a wanted man and a battle soon erupted between English first division clubs Arsenal and Manchester Utd for the wily Scotsman's services. Arsenal stated that a gentleman's agreement had already been reached between the two parties before the World Cup had even kicked off. Manchester Utd were ready to offer him whatever he wanted to get him to Old Trafford and tried their best to sabotage the deal, but on the 1st of August 1986 Ferguson proved that he was a man of his word, and he put pen to paper on a five year deal to manage Arsenal.

Ferguson's right hand man at Highbury would be fellow Scotsman, George Graham, who had also been considered for the top job. The fact that Graham, who was already something of an Arsenal legend after playing 227 games for the club, had been overlooked instantly brought unwanted tensions into the dressing room. Rumours were rife that the pair couldn't agree on anything, and training ground arguments about tactics, signings and training schedules were all too common.

The 1986-87 season was a mitigated disaster as The Gunners narrowly avoided relegation by beating Norwich City 1-0 at Highbury on the final day of the season. The next year did see some improvement though, beginning with Arsenal beating title favourites Liverpool on the opening day of the season 3-0. They even broke in to the top two in November after a fantastic 3-1 victory over Chelsea. But the good times were short lived and after Arsenal were unceremoniously dumped out of the FA Cup in the third round, the two fiery Scotsmen clashed in the dressing room.

The fight between the two has taken on legendary status in the world of football. People talk more about it than any heavy weight boxing match in history. Who won the league that year is insignificant, because what people really wanted to know was who threw the first punch. The story goes that Ferguson was unhappy with his assistant who pushed the side to defend the 1-0 half time lead that they had secured. Ferguson on the other hand, wanted his team to go out and finish the job. The resultant half time argument sent the players out on to the field with more than a few mixed messages, and they were eventually overrun, losing the game 4-1. As the team entered the dressing room after the game, Alex Ferguson kicked a boot that was lying on the floor towards George Graham. The boot hit him flush on the nose breaking it in two places. Graham understandably flew into a fit of rage and wrestled his boss to the ground smashing his head on the floor. With both men bleeding on the ground, the fight began to turn a little nasty. With neither of them gaining the upper hand, Graham rammed his thumb into Ferguson's eye. Ferguson's response was to grab Graham by the nuts and squeeze as hard as he could. Graham's girly scream was heard by the press who were now trying to break down the door to see what was going on. The Arsenal players tried their best to keep them out but it was of no use, and the press finally broke through. When they did, they found Ferguson allegedly kicking Graham in the back, before spitting on his head and saying "This is for talking me out of signing Bryan Robson, you gutless prick". Pictures of the pair unceremoniously rolling around on the floor were spread all over the world giving the Arsenal board no choice but to sack them both. On top of their dismissal, the FA got their two pence worth, fining them 10,000 GBP each for bringing the game into disrepute.

Despite leaving Arsenal in disgrace they both quickly made returns to football and with great success. George Graham took over the hot seat at Manchester Utd, while Alex Ferguson went back north of the border to former club, Glasgow Rangers. Graham succeeded in bringing some of the glory days back to Old Trafford, and in 1989 they lifted the League title for the first time since 1967, beating Liverpool on goal difference. But in 1992 Graham was forced to resign to fight a possible jail term after allegations arose about illegal transfer moves. He would escape conviction, but he never managed again.

Alex Ferguson won 4 Scottish League titles and two Scottish cups in his four year stint at Glasgow Rangers before deciding the time was right to prove himself back in England. On 27th July 1992 Alex Ferguson took over the vacant position at Manchester Utd. In the press conference set up to announce the appointment Ferguson took one last swipe at his former partner, George Graham, by claiming, "It could take years to clean up the mess that he has left."

Ferguson's first act in charge was to promote a youngster by the name of Ryan Gigs into the first team, before buying the volatile but brilliant talent of Frenchman Eric Cantona for just 1.2 million GBP. Manchester Utd would go on to win the newly formed English Premier League in 1993 and, with Ferguson in charge, they would dominate English football for the next 15 years.

Alex Ferguson and the One That Got Away

OVER THE YEARS SIR ALEX FERGUSON HAS MANAGED SOME of the greatest players in the world. David Beckham, Eric Cantona, Bryan Robson, Roy Keane and Ruud Van Nistelrooy are to name but a few. But if Sir Alex had had his way this seemingly endless list would also include the likes of Ronaldinho, Peter Beardsley, Fernando Torres and Matthew Le Tissier. There are two players in particular that Ferguson would have given his right testicle to have at Old Trafford. He was disappointed on two separate occasions to sign one, while the man himself admits that his failure to sign the other is the biggest regret of his career.

Alan Shearer

ALAN SHEARER IS AN ENGLAND GOAL SCORING LEGEND. His performance in the 1996 European Championships will go down in history alongside Geoff Hurst's 1966 World Cup display, Gary Lineker's in Mexico 1986 and Paul Gascoigne's in Italia 90 as one of the greatest ever England performances. On top of this, he is Newcastle Utd's record goal scorer with 303 goals and the English Premier League's greatest marksman with 261.

Ever since he made his debut for Southampton on 26th March, 1988 he has been a defender's worst nightmare thanks mainly to his strength, a great turn of pace and devastating right foot. In just his second first team outing, Shearer would announce his arrival to the football world in style. At just 17 years and 240 days he became the youngest player to score a hat-trick in top flight English football, beating the 30 year old record held by Jimmy Greaves. But he didn't stop there, and after 23 goals in 118 appearances for Southampton, and 13 goals in only 11 England U21 games, the top clubs of English football were drooling over the young striker. At the end of the 1991 -92 season Shearer's time at The Dell seemed well and truly over and two clubs, Blackburn Rovers and Manchester Utd, would go on to fight it out for his signature.

Blackburn Rovers had come from nowhere to dominate the football landscape after a steel tycoon by the name of Jack Walker started investing millions of pounds into the small Lancashire club. He had already persuaded Liverpool legend Kenny Dalglish out of retirement to manage the team, while Walker splashed the cash on big name players such as Mike Newell. The hope was that Blackburn would buy their way into England's elite, and, as Walker himself said, make clubs such as Manchester Utd look "cheap" in the process.

The rise of Blackburn Rovers with King Kenny leading the way and Jack Walker signing the cheques was truly phenomenal. They quickly went from a struggling 1st division side to being promoted to the Premier League in 1992 and were looking to cement their place in the top flight when Jack Walker lived up to his word and splashed out over 3 million GBP to secure the services of Shearer, a fee that Manchester Utd simply couldn't match.

Shearer would go on to help Blackburn win the premiership title in 1995. But just a year later after his sublime performances in Euro 96 it looked like he would once again be on the move with Man Utd boss, Alex Ferguson, favourite to finally get his man. The pair met on several occasions and a deal looked done, but at the last moment the deal collapsed and Shearer moved back to his home town joined Newcastle Utd instead for a world record fee of 15 million GBP. The reason behind the collapsed move to Manchester has never been revealed but there are two very popular theories. (all of this part had been missing for some reason.

1. Shearer and Cantona

EVERYONE KNOWS THAT SHEARER WAS PARTIAL TO taking penalties; in fact he used to have it drawn into his contract that no one else could take one without his say so. But in 1996 this small contract clause proved to be his undoing when trying to secure a dream move to Manchester Utd. During a meeting with Alex Ferguson, with a deal almost done, Alan Shearer brought up the subject of penalties and mentioned that he would expect to be the penalty taker at Old Trafford. Ferguson quickly pointed out that a certain Frenchman by the name of Eric Cantona was already taking the penalties, but said that he would ask him to give up the spot. There was no poetic response about trawlers and seagulls this time. In fact, Cantona's response can probably be translated as, "Tell Alan to go fuck himself." With that, the deal fell through, and Ferguson missed out on forming what could have been one of the greatest ever strike partnerships.

2. Jack Walker

MANCHESTER UTD HAD BEEN TRYING THEIR BEST TO unsettle Shearer throughout the 1995-96 season by undermining his current club Blackburn Rovers. And as the Euro 96 championships came to an end it looked as though their plans may have worked as Alan Shearer looked set to leave Ewood Park, despite the best attempts of Jack Walker to keep him at the club. But there was one thing that Alex Ferguson and the Old Trafford board hadn't considered: Jack Walker's pure hatred of Manchester Utd. In 1996, Jack Walker showed that his earlier statement about making Manchester Utd look cheap was no publicity stunt as he refused to accept any bid put forward by Alex Ferguson's club even if it did mean missing out on a few million pounds. So, in July 1996, Walker rejected Manchester Utd's bid, and accepted the lesser 15 million GBP offer from Newcastle.

Personally I prefer the first story.

What If?

THERE WERE FEARS THAT ALAN SHEARER'S RECORD breaking move to Manchester Utd could fall through after an interview by Utd star Eric Cantona appeared in Britain's Daily Star newspaper. Asked if he was excited by Shearer's imminent arrival at Old Trafford, Cantona labelled the England international as an, "overrated lump that uses his elbows more than his feet." Cantona went on to say, "Shearer will never take a penalty if he joins Utd," and he "should feel privileged," to be considered good enough to play in the same side as himself.

Shearer was reportedly furious with the interview, especially with the fact that Alex Ferguson had promised him the penalty taking duties and vowed to never play for Utd while Cantona was at the club.

The Blackburn board was not happy with Shearer's decision as they were hoping to cash in on the star striker, and refused to let him play in the first team. Shearer would languish in the reserves for nearly three months and was regularly booed by the home fans.

During this time, Eric Cantona's form suffered greatly under the constant speculation that he may have to leave the club for Ferguson to net Shearer. With Cantona not quite at his best, Utd struggled, and after a 3-1 defeat by Liverpool on 12th October 1996 they slipped to sixth place in the league.

Frustrated at playing reserve team football, Alan Shearer finally caved in and agreed to share the penalty kicks with Eric Cantona and signed a three year Old Trafford deal on 27th October 1996 for a record 17.5 million GBP, vowing that the world had seen nothing of his abilities to date.

His first game was against Chelsea on 2nd November. The Cantona- Shearer partnership showed flashes of potential early on, but an argument between the two soon erupted after Shearer was brought down in the box and Utd were awarded a penalty. Whilst Shearer received treatment for an ankle knock, Cantona scooped up the ball and placed it on the spot. Once Shearer had got to his feet and realized that Eric was set to take the kick he shouted something toward his team mate. Whatever it was, it seemed to anger the Frenchman who spat in Shearer's general direction before sliding the ball into the bottom corner. The argument seemed to continue and just five minutes later, boss Alex Ferguson pulled the pair from the pitch, and in the post game press conference labelled them as "immature". A mass of transfer rumours followed with Real Madrid, and AC Milan sniffing around, as both Shearer and Cantona were left out of the squad and told to grow up or leave Old Trafford. Just as it looked likely that they would be sold on, Ferguson decided to give them one last chance and recalled them for the game against Tottenham on 12th January 1997. Utd, which was struggling in 7th place in the table looked like a different side with the two star strikers back in the side.

After just 10 minutes Cantona picked up the ball on the left and cut inside on to his right foot. The Frenchman looked set to unleash a shot when he played a clever little flick in behind the Tottenham defence. Shearer was the first to react and without even breaking stride he lashed the ball into the back of the net. Utd won the game 5-1 and finished the season strongly climbing to third in the league just seven points behind eventual champions, Newcastle.

In the last half of the season the Shearer, Cantona partnership amassed an amazing 31 goals. But the partnership was brought to an abrupt end when Cantona retired from the sport in May 1997, leaving the world wondering what the pair could have achieved.

Paul Gascoigne

PAUL GASCOIGNE PLAYED HIS WAY INTO THE HEARTS of all Englishmen with his superb performances during the Italia 90 World Cup. The whole of England was with him as he shed tears at the semi final stage after receiving a yellow card that meant he would miss the final. And the whole of England supported him through every injury, every visit to rehab and every transgression with the law. But despite their love of the great man, the English football faithful can't help but look back on the career of Paul Gascoigne and see it as a massive waste of talent.

The Paul Gascoigne story began on the 13th of April

1985 when he came on as substitute for Newcastle Utd against Queens Park Rangers. He soon became a focal point for opposing managers who would try anything to keep him out of the game. But one of the more interesting man marking jobs was undertaken by Wimbledon midfielder Vinnie Jones, and immortalized in an iconic photograph. The picture shows Jones, with anger ripped across his face, helping himself to a handful of Gascoigne's nuts while Gascoigne winces with pain. From here, his rise was swift and it wasn't long before he began to attract attention from the likes of Liverpool, Manchester Utd and Tottenham Hotspur. But Gascoigne was born and bred in the North East and was reluctant to leave. By the end of the 1987-88 season though, he was becoming a little disheartened by the club, feeling that they lacked direction and felt that a move was necessary to further his international ambitions.

Gascoigne apparently had his heart set on a move to Liverpool which was the dominant force in English football at the time, but Liverpool manager Kenny Dalglish was reluctant to put in a solid bid believing that Gascoigne wouldn't add anything to his already star packed side. Both Tottenham and Manchester Utd saw Gazza as the perfect acquisition. After many discussions and a lot of thought it was the persuasiveness of Manchester Utd manager Alex Ferguson that seemed to win out.

"We spoke to him the night before I went on holiday. He says, 'Go and enjoy yourself, Mr Ferguson,' I will be signing for Manchester Utd.' So I went on my holidays," remembers Sir Alex in an interview with the Daily Mail newspaper. "But the chairman rang and said, "I've got some bad news – He signed for Tottenham. They bought a house for his mother and father in the North East and that swung it."

While the amazing u turn didn't seem to damage Gascoigne's career in the short term, many people feel that if he had moved to Manchester many of the demons that made sure he never reached his full potential could have been stamped out of him under the tutelage of the great Sir Alex Ferguson. Even Gascoigne admits that he probably should have stuck to his deal.

"Maybe if I had stayed at Man U I might have still been there," Gascoigne is quoted as saying in *The Daily Mirror Newspaper*. "I don't know, you just look at these players and the squad of young kids that play, Rooney that's there, the Neville brothers and 'Becks', the way he just brought them on and there are so many. It took me six years to get back talking to Sir Alex. I called him from Lazio and asked him would he sign us. He was with Eric Cantona and he said he would see what Eric Cantona was going to do, but I think everyone knows if you do something to Sir Alex Ferguson the way I did, you don't get a second chance."

What If?

DESPITE THE BEST ATTEMPTS OF TOTTENHAM HOTSPUR to bag him, Paul Gascoigne joined the revolution taking place at Manchester Utd on the 26th of June 1988. Utd manager Alex Ferguson was delighted with his new acquisition, labelling him as "the best young talent in the world" and "the key to league title success." It was a big billing for such a young player to live up to, but rather than shy away from the spotlight, Paul Gascoigne relished the challenge, and showed in his first game exactly what Manchester Utd fans could expect from their new signing.

It was 27th August 1988 and the unsuspecting victims of the new look Utd side were Queens Park Rangers who were looking to build on their very respectable fourth place finish the season before. But from the very first whistle there was only one team in it as Paul Gascoigne and his new midfield partner, Bryan Robson, took total control of the game, with Gascoigne showing a maturity and work ethic that many had seen to be missing from his performances at Newcastle. After some sustained pressure, though, it was Mark Hughes who was starting his second spell at Utd after a disappointing time at Barcelona that got the breakthrough. Gascoigne picked the ball up on the edge of his own area and went on a driving run forward. The pitch seemed to open for the youngster as runs from Brian Mclair and Mark Robbins took defenders out of the picture. Gascoigne strolled into the QPR half unchallenged and looked like he might try and go all the way. But he glanced up just in time to see Lee Sharpe haring down the left. He picked him out with a beautiful cross field ball that landed right in Sharpe's path. Sharpe crossed the ball first time into the box. Mark Hughes made a diagonal run toward the near post and headed the ball into the bottom corner. Although it had been Hughes who had scored the breakthrough goal it was new boy Paul Gascoigne that got all the praise, and everyone in the stadium could see why. A new era of Utd success was brewing.

Gascoigne capped his man of the match performance with a goal in the 87th minute, albeit a tap in from two yards out, to seal a 3-0 victory. Throughout the season Utd proved that on their day they were a match for anyone. Following their stunning opening win, they travelled to Anfield to face the defending champions, Liverpool. Liverpool shot out to an early 2-0 lead but in the second half Utd clicked into gear and two goals from Mark Hughes levelled the score giving Liverpool a big scare. They also did the double over Arsenal, but it was defeats against the likes of Charlton and Luton that saw them finish third and seven points behind eventual champions, Liverpool.

But in the 1989-90 season Utd would make no such

mistakes. Paul Gascoigne's form saw him become the PFA Player of the year as he scored 25 goals and dominated in almost every game he played. It was on 14th April 1990 in a game against QPR, the team he had made his debut against nearly two years earlier, however, that Gascoigne became a true Manchester Utd legend. Utd needed to win to clinch their first title since 1967, but as the team stood on the edge of greatness it was obvious that many of them were wracked with nerves. Mistakes were made and after one too many sloppy passes QPR forward Les Ferdinand capitalised and slotted the ball past Utd keeper, Jim Leighton, to give his side the lead after 20 minutes.

The goal only spurred Utd, and especially Paul Gascoigne, into action. Just ten minutes after QPR had taken the lead, Utd were awarded a free kick about 40 yards from goal. As the Rangers players sorted out the wall and who was marking who, Gascoigne took the kick quickly, chipping the ball into an unguarded net. The Rangers players protested that they had not heard the whistle but the goal stood and Utd were now flying. QPR survived until half time, but just five minutes after the break, Gazza was at it again. He picked up the ball on the right and cut inside, letting fly with a left foot thunder bolt that crashed off the underside of the bar and into the net to give Utd the lead. Gascoigne sealed the victory and the league title just ten minutes before the end with his and Utd's third after a header from a Lee Sharpe corner. The English football press were full of praise for Alex Ferguson's side and especially Paul Gascoigne who they were now labelling as England's talisman for the upcoming World Cup in Italy. Little did they know that the new empire Alex Ferguson was trying to build was about to come crashing down around his feet in spectacular fashion.

It all began after Utd's final game of the season. They had beaten Charlton Athletic 3-0 and paraded their new trophy in front of their home fans. There was something of a party atmosphere in the dressing room as everyone involved in the club from the chairman to the tea lady was squashed in there, sipping on champagne, or, as in the case of Paul Gascoigne, swigging it from the bottle. Gazza had been on his best behaviour since his move to Manchester, but now he was intent on letting his hair down. He slinked the last of his bottle of champers and went over to his boss to thank him for supporting his career and turning him into the devastating player he had become. Alex Ferguson was just as thankful to his young protégé, and thought that a farewell drink between the two was just what the doctor ordered. Gascoigne and Ferguson were last seen leaving the dressing room and heading towards Ferguson's office, but from there the exact events of the night are unknown. Even Gazza himself was unsure what went down as he tried his best to remember during an interview with *The Guardian* newspaper in 2002.

"The Gaffer asked if I fancied having a little glass of whisky with him before I left for Italy. I was already half cut when we got to his office and he pulled out a bottle he had bought ten years ago and was saving for a special occasion. I honestly don't remember much past the fifth glass apart from mentioning it could be a laugh heading into town."

At four o'clock the next morning, two members of the Manchester Police were shocked when they discovered a man crumpled in a heap on the floor of Shambles Square, apparently pantless.

"John looked at me and said, "I think that's Alex Ferguson,' " said Constable James Peterson in an interview with *Four Four Two* magazine in 2005. "I just thought it was some homeless guy and went over to see if he was OK. When I got closer I could hear him mumbling something about Gazza and how he wished he had pictures of Kenny

Dalglish dressed in pink six inch stilettos and a yellow feather boa so that he could bribe him into selling John Barnes. It was only then that I realised it actually was Alex Ferguson, and he was wearing no pants."

The two officers covered him up and took him to the local station where he was charged for being drunk and disorderly and for indecent exposure. Gascoigne escaped arrest as he disappeared for two days, finally showing up in a pub near his parent's home in Newcastle, but by then the rumours of their night out had hit the newsstands and claims of drug taking, strip bar orgies and naked swimming in the River Irwell were rife. Gazza tried to laugh it off but after pictures of the two wearing nothing but bow ties snorting some sort of white powder off the bar in a well known Manchester strip bar, England boss Bobby Robson had no choice but drop him from his squad for the World Cup. The Manchester board tried their best to stand strong behind Ferguson, the man that had brought them their first league title in over 20 years, and their star player. But after the English FA handed out two year bans for both, they had no choice but to terminate their contracts.

Gascoigne spent the next year in an exclusive American rehab centre and, amazingly, came back to football in 1993 when Newcastle boss Kevin Keegan brought him back to his home town club. He never reached the heights expected of him in his early career and the English football press still tend to look back on the life of Paul Gascoigne with a wistful sigh at what could have been.

Ferguson became a total recluse after being sacked by Manchester Utd. There were many attempts from various clubs to bring him out of retirement but he always gracefully declined. That was until 2009, when his old pal Paul Gascoigne came knocking on his door begging him to come and help save Newcastle Utd from relegation. Ferguson saw that the time was right to redeem himself in the eyes of the footballing public, and took the Newcastle hot seat with just seven games remaining in the 2008 – 2009 season. Utd were second from the bottom, seven points away from safety and in desperate need of a miracle, which Ferguson delivered. They went on to win five and draw the other two, easily avoiding the drop. After a stunning start with Newcastle to the 2009 -2010 season, Ferguson was once again one of the most wanted football managers in the world with newly mega rich Manchester City looking to poach him after they sacked manager Mark Hughes in December. On the second of January 2010 Ferguson angered his former club and his current one when he took over at City and hailed them as "the biggest club in English football." But he soon backed up his words winning his first five games in charge including a stunning 7-1 victory away to Stoke City on the 26th of January. The future looked bright for City.

Liverpool's Danish Bacon

IN THE LATE 1970S AND EARLY 1980S, ENGLISH CLUBS were dominating European football. Or should I say that in the late 1970s and early 1980s Liverpool FC were totally dominating European football? Between 1977 and 1984 the Merseyside club went on an unbelievable run, winning the European Cup an amazing four times making them the most feared team in the world and the Club that every up and coming player wanted to play for; apart, it seems, from the Danish wizard, Michael Laudrup.

Along with Lurpak Bacon, Carlsberg and Peter Schmeichal there is no doubt that Michael Laudrup is one of Denmark's greatest ever exports. In 1983, as a 19 year old, he was already creating waves within the football world playing for Danish club, Brondby. He was an attacking midfielder with great vision and flair who also looked totally calm and composed every time he was on the ball. He was later called "The Genius" by Real Madrid team mate Ivan Zamorano who had 82% of his goals in the 1994-95 season created by the great man. While his silky skills have also led to the Spanish saying of "Made in Laudrup," used whenever a player skips past a defender leaving him scratching around in the dirt like a dying duck, or Eric Djemba Djemba, whichever description fits best.

After scoring nearly a goal a game for Brondby the fight for the most promising talent in the world came down to two of the world's top clubs, the reigning Italian Serie A Champions, Juventus, and the three time European Champions, Liverpool. Liverpool saw the player as a perfect readymade replacement for Kenny Dalglish, who, at 32, had only a couple more years left in him. Laudrup was also keen to join such a prestigious club, and in the summer of 1983 a three year deal was agreed to bring the talented Dane to Anfield. But just as quickly as the deal seemed to have been done, it collapsed after the Liverpool board decided that they wanted to secure the player for four years, not three. Laudrup was simply not willing to pledge so much of his future so early on in his career and he signed for Juventus instead.

Missing out on such a precocious talent didn't seem to hamper Liverpool at all, who went on to win their fourth European title in 1984. The collapse of the move also did not affect Laudrup either, who went on to have amazing success with Juventus, Barcelona and Real Madrid. But what would have happened if the move had been allowed to go through?

What If?

LIVERPOOL SIGNED THE AMAZING DANISH PROSPECT, Michael Laudrup on the 30th July 1983 for around 300,000 GBP in the hope that he would one day assume the role of Kop hero, currently taken by Scotsman, Kenny Dalglish. Not many people thought that the transition would be an instant one, and believed that the 19 year old Laudrup would have to be content with spending a few seasons getting splinters in his arse as he watched and learned from the man he had been signed to replace. And for the first six months of the 1983-1984 season it looked as though that was exactly how things would be going. Laudrup made a few cameo appearances as a substitute and even scored a goal after a rare start against Sunderland in September, but it would be a freak training ground accident that would see him thrown into the deep end.

It was 4th January 1984 and the squad was being put through its paces in one the many five aside games that were a regular part of the team's training. Laudrup and Dalglish were put on opposite teams, and as Laudrup was always looking to impress, and Dalglish wanted to show the management that he still had what it takes, a fierce battle between the two erupted. It started off as a light hearted tit for tat type of argument, but as Laudrup began to dictate to his senior opponent the frustration began to tell on Daglish's face. And after the young pretender slipped the ball through his legs and smashed it into the net for yet another goal, Dalglish snapped. As the rest of the players praised Laudrup for his silky skills, King Kenny felt that his Liverpool career was beginning to disappear down the drain. He kicked off his boots, left the pitch and didn't even go into the dressing room for a shower; instead he headed straight for his car. Still full of anger and frustration, Kenny Dalglish pulled out of the car park and sped away without looking. The driver that side swiped Dalglish didn't have a prayer of avoiding the collision, but being a Liverpool fan he was certainly full of remorse.

"I couldn't believe it when I saw who was in the other car," said Colin Keenan in a 1999 interview with *The Telegraph* newspaper. "He was unconscious and bleeding from the head. I fell down to the ground crying like a baby, I thought I had just killed Kenny Dalglish."

In reality, Dalglish wasn't dead, but he had broken his leg in two places ruling him out for the rest of the season. It was a massive disappointment for the Liverpool fans, but little did they know that a new era was about to begin at Anfield.

Liverpool's first game without Dalglish would be at home against Wolverhampton Wanderers on 14th January 1984. Rumours that a training ground spat between Dalglish and Laudrup had caused the Dalglish injury filtered through to the fans, and they unceremoniously booed the young Dane as he walked out onto the pitch. Many players would have totally crumbled under the pressure, but after just 7 minutes it was evident that Michael Laudrup wasn't going to give up so easily. He picked the ball up on Liverpool's right hand side, and looked up as if he was going to play it down the line. Instead, he flicked the ball the opposite way into the path of a marauding Graeme Souness who produced a defence splitting pass for Ian Rush to lash home the first goal of the day. From there, Liverpool and Laudrup were unstoppable as they thumped a hapless Wolverhampton team 5-1 with 'The Great Dane' creating three and scoring the fifth, chipping the goal keeper from just inside his own half. The fans that had packed into the Kop to openly boo Michael Laudrup for his part in the Dalglish injury were blown away by his performance and were left wondering whether Kenny would make it back into the starting line-up.

Liverpool went on to win the League by an amazing 20 points, and to beat Roma in the European Cup final 3-0 with Laudrup being the key to everything good that his side produced. Watching this success from the sidelines, Kenny Dalglish became convinced that his time at Anfield was up and on the 1st of May 1984 he handed in a formal transfer request. After fully recovering from his injuries, Kenny Dalglish moved back to the club where he started his career, Celtic, stating that he thought his "first team opportunities" would be restricted with the emergence of such a "world class talent" in Michael Laudrup. He spent two successful seasons as a player before becoming the club's manager in 1986.

For Liverpool, the loss of Dalglish was soon followed by the loss of both his replacement and manager. After a riot at the 1985 European Cup final between Liverpool and Juventus resulted in the death of 39 fans, Liverpool was banned from European competition. Laudrup felt that to become one of the greatest players in the world he would have to continue playing at the top level and demanded that the club sell him on. It was Spanish giants Real Madrid that coughed up the 2 million GBP asking price, but the money was no comfort to a side that had now lost two of its best players as well as its manager, Joe Fagan, who quit soon after the ill fated game.

Liverpool gave fiery midfielder, Graeme Souness, the managerial role in August 1985, but after a disappointing season in which the club failed to win a trophy and finished 4th in the league he was sacked. Souness was soon replaced by his fellow countryman and former Scotland manager, Alex Ferguson. The move came as a surprise to many as Ferguson had been set to join Manchester Utd, but when Liverpool had come calling, he just couldn't resist.

"Liverpool was the biggest club in Europe," said Ferguson after quitting the club in 2001. "When I was asked to become the Liverpool manager I was just honoured to even be considered. It was really an easy decision."

Ferguson won the league in his first season in charge and helped Liverpool continue their dominance of the English game for the next 15 years.

Did You Ever Have Your Head Up Your Big Fat Arse?

Harry Redknapp

HARRY REDKNAPP IS WELL KNOWN FOR HIS fantastic dealings in the transfer market. For years he managed West Ham on a shoe string budget, pulling talent out from unknown clubs and countries while bringing the best out of players who seemed to be no better than average at other clubs. His skills have even seen him take Portsmouth from a struggling lower league club to one winning the FA Cup and regularly challenging for a spot in Europe. But as the saying goes, "Everyone makes mistakes," and big 'arry Redknapp has made a couple of howlers that could send the man crazier than a coconut when he finally gets to sit back in his rocking chair and contemplate his career.

It was the mid eighties and Harry Redknapp was in charge of Bournemouth. The club was short of cash and, as usual, Big Arry was on the lookout for a bargain. He decided to go and watch a non league game as he had heard rumours of a dynamic forward playing for Enfield that could make the step up to play professional football. It turned out that the rumours had been correct and Harry

Redknapp instantly signed Carl Richards, paying him a
measly 220 GBP a week. Bournemouth fans still see
Richards as a bit of a legend at the club as his two year spell
saw him score 16 goals in 71 games, which helped them
achieve promotion to division two. Richards was then sold
for 80,000 GBP all of which was profit, making the whole
affair very profitable for the club. But rather than praising
Harry for this seemingly genius little bit of business,
Bournemouth fans should be making effigies of their former
manager, hanging them from lampposts and setting them on
fire, because Redknapp, the king of the transfer market,
failed to spot another player playing in the same Enfield
side as Richards.

"I remember one bank holiday Monday, I and my wife,
Sandra, fancied a day out," says Redknapp looking back on
the incident in an interview with Britain's *Daily Mail*
newspaper. "So I told her I was going to Nuneaton to
watch a centre forward called Carl Richards, a big,
handsome boy that looked like Carl Lewis – and ran like
him too. I called him over after the game. He had never
heard of me, but I told him I would sign him, offered him
220 GBP a week and went to see his manager to do a deal
with Enfield. While I was waiting, Carl's mate came up to
me and said 'Don't sign him, sign me. I am a much better
player.' I signed Carl and ignored his mate who turned out
to be Ian Wright."

Ian Wright had already failed in trials at several other
clubs so Harry wasn't the only person that failed to spot
the precocious talent, but I am sure that won't be any
comfort when he is washing down the last of a box of
sleeping pills with a bottle of cheap Russian vodka.

Missing out on Ian Wright will certainly be one of
Harry Redknapp's biggest regrets but you have to say that
it probably won't be the biggest. After managing
Bournemouth with great success, Redknapp went on to

become boss of Premier League side West Ham Utd, which he had played for in the late 1960's and early 1970's. While he was there, Redknapp managed to sell or buy an average of 19 players a season, and keep them in the top flight with little more than a packet of joo joo beans as funds. In 1994 his scouting arms were stretching out to Eastern Europe and a few players were picked out to have trials at Upton Park. One, in particular, was raved about and even got a chance to play in the West Ham reserves against Barnet where he scored a goal. But Big Arry wasn't impressed and even less so with the 1 million GBP price tag. "He didn't look like anything special at all, and I sent him back and told my contacts out there to get me a better player," said Redknapp. But that kid who didn't look anything special was none other than future AC Milan superstar, Andriy Shevchenko. Sheva has since denied that any such trial took place, but if it is true, Harry, I am sure there is a long piece of rope in your shed that should do the trick.

But we shouldn't only pick on Harry Redknapp because he is not the only manager that has managed to get his head stuck up his arse, and miss out on some of the world's greatest football talent.

Bill Shankly

THE LEGEND THAT IS BILL SHANKLY HELPED BUILD ONE of the biggest clubs in the world of football, Liverpool FC. When Shanks took over, Liverpool was nothing more than a mid table second division team with little prospects of climbing to the heights that are now expected every season at Anfield. Shanks brought in players such as Ian St John and Ron Yates and the club was soon promoted and challenging for major honours. But Shankly has proved that even the best managers of all time have moments of madness or days when they really should have stayed in bed. During one of those days in the mid 60s, Shanks told a young Scotsman that he was not good enough to play for Liverpool. It just happened to be none other than Kenny Dalglish. Dalglish had come south of the border to try and find himself a club but after he failed in trials at West Ham and Liverpool he returned north. His real dream was to sign for the team he had supported all his life, Glasgow Rangers, but it was their arch rivals, Celtic, that finally spotted what so many others had missed, and after he had established himself as a world class talent playing in the green and white hoops, Liverpool was forced to fork out a British record 440,000 GBP for his services in 1977. Dalglish went on to become a legend at the club and was placed first in Liverpool's list of 100 players that shook the kop, but the legend could have started a lot earlier if only Shanks could have got out of the right side of the bed that day.

Sir Bobby Robson

SIR BOBBY ROBSON WAS KNOWN WITHIN THE WORLD of football as a total gentleman and an amazing tactician with a superb eye for talent. Over the years he has turned teenagers such as Brazilian superstar Ronaldo, who became a world cup winner and won the world player of the year award three times, Portuguese legend Figo, Ruud Van Nistelrooy, Mick Mills, John Wark, and Alan Brazil as well as current England stars Jermaine Jenas and James Milner, into superstars.

While Sir Bobby was manager at Ipswich Town, however, he had a few days that I am sure won't be remembered as his best. We all know that Robson was a massive Paul Gascoigne fan and was a positive influence in the career of the England legend. It was Robson that called

Gascoigne up to the England squad in 1988 when he was just 21 and made him a key player in the England team that reached the semi final stage of the 1990 World Cup. But one day in 1981 a fourteen year old Gascoigne was doing the rounds of some of the big English clubs trying to find himself a professional contract when he landed on the front steps at Ipswich Town. Despite thinking that Gascoigne had some talent Robson was concerned about the youngster's weight and told him that he would never make it as a pro unless he shed a few pounds. Gascoigne made his debut for Newcastle Utd just four years later against Queens Park Rangers and went on to become one of England's greatest ever players. DOH!

But the Bobby Robson fuck ups don't stop there, because he apparently also told John Barnes and Dutch maestro Ruud Gullit that they weren't good enough to play for Ipswich. Yes, you read right, not good enough to play for Ipswich. He later said that neither of them had the skills at that stage of their career, but I am sure that he was kicking himself pretty hard on the inside once Gullit had signed for AC Milan and Barnes was tearing defenders' arse holes while at Liverpool.

Atletico Madrid

DESPITE THE LIKES OF SHANKLY AND REDKNAPP making some shocking decisions throughout the years, by far the worst has to be the one made by Spanish club Atletico Madrid in 1989.

The club was struggling financially at that stage and some drastic action was needed to keep the club afloat. The then chairman, Jesús Gil, decided that closing down the club's youth system and releasing the coaches and players would save them some pennies and secure the short term future of the club. But just five years later one of those youth players released by Atletico made his debut for their cross town rivals Real. At just seventeen years and four months he was the club's youngest ever player and went on to become their greatest ever goal scorer as well as the first player to score 50 goals in the European Champions League. That player was Raúl González.

Nice thinking, Mr Gil. Your great insight has ensured that Atletico will always be known as the second team in Madrid.

Emanuel Adebayour

SOMETIMES, AS A MANAGER YOU HAVE TO PUT UP WITH a know it all chairman who does nothing but rain on your parade, even when you know that you have uncovered something of a special talent. Just ask Gordon Strachan.

In 2003, while Strachan was managing Southampton he spotted a young striker playing for Metz in France, Emmanuel Adebayour. Talks took place between the two, a fee was agreed with Metz and it looked as though the Togo international would be moving to the South of England, only for Southampton Chairman Rupert Lowe to give his manager a swift kick in the knackers, refusing to give him the cash. Southampton fans now look at what Adebayour has gone on to achieve and are understandably furious that their chairman didn't have the balls to spend the money that could have seen The Saints become one of England's top clubs. And if you are a Southampton fan hearing this news for the first time, and are thinking of hiring a hit man to take down Lowe as he picks up his morning paper while wearing his Versace loafers, maybe you should skip to the next page, because deals that apparently would have brought Dider Drogba, Steed Malbranque and Louis Saha to the club all suffered the same fate.

Rupert Lowe's inept running of the Southampton Football Club didn't end by showing his lack of bollocks in the transfer market, because he also made some dodgy decisions when it came to his choice of men to manage the team.

The Premier Leagues Worst Ever Managers

Southampton and Rupert Lowe

STUART GRAY HAD A LESS THAN SPECTACULAR PLAYING career that he carried over into management. After undertaking a number of different coaching roles with various clubs, he was given the opportunity of managing in the big time by Southampton Chairman Rupert Lowe in 2001. The arrangement lasted just 19 matches, with Southampton winning only 6 games in that time, before Lowe realized his mistake and replaced him with Gordon Strachan. To impound the fact that Stuart Gray has no idea how to run a football team he was sacked by Northampton Town in 2009 after guiding the club to relegation from League 1.

But Rupert Lowe's terrible choice of managers didn't end there and in 2004 he went into overdrive.

Paul Sturrock was brought in on the 4th of March 2004 from Plymouth Argyle, where he had been named the club's manager of the century. The award did nothing to excite Saints fans who thought that Chairman Rupert Lowe had hired Sturrock hoping that he would perform badly, thus comforting the blow when the much hated Glen Hoddle once again took over. Whatever the reasons behind the appointment, it only lasted six months when the players realized that he was never going to have the ability to manage in the Premier League, and demanded his sacking. Rupert had caved in to his players' whims, but he continued his string of poor appointments by naming Steve Wigley as Storrock's replacement. The question marks surrounding the appointment of Wigley were instant. The Southampton fans were not impressed by it, but although they only had to wait 14 games before he was sacked, they were still left scratching their heads after Rupert Lowe appointed a well known rugby coach as the club's director of football. Sir Clive Woodward had won the Rugby Union World Cup as the coach of England in 2003 and instantly set out his intentions to coach in football.

Most people laughed off the suggestion that he could make the step across, but Lowe thought that having such a successful man at the club could prove to be a great motivation to his players. But when Big 'arry Redknapp took control of The Saints he found the presence of Woodward to be nothing more than an unnecessary distraction, saying, "He is coming to learn (football). He is coming to pick people's brains and I am happy with that. But I am the manager and I recommend the players."

On the 31st of August 2006 the Southampton board informed the British press that Clive Woodward no longer worked at the club.

Despite Southampton's long list of terrible managers they have by no means cornered the crap manager market.

David O'Leary

THERE WILL BE A LOT OF PEOPLE OUT THERE WONDERING how on earth I can put a man who has guided a team to the Champions League Semi Final in a list of the Premier

League's worst ever managers. For a man who has never even been close to relegation, and who did such a sterling job of keeping Aston Villa as a mid table team for so many years, surely this is sacrilege; surely there are worse managers than him. And look, you're probably right, but the truth is that Mr O'Leary has never taken the flack that he more than deserves for the downfall of Leeds Utd. He was in charge of it all, the signings, the tactics and general running of the club. Yes, Peter Ridsdale began selling off players left right and centre, but this only came after he had done what so many other chairman fail to do, he put dangled his love spuds in the lions mouth and then whipped it with a wet towel. After Leeds had been knocked out of Champions League at the semi final stage by Valencia, O'Leary asked his Chairman for a hefty transfer kitty to help him make that next step up. To help Leeds become one of Europe's elite clubs, O'Leary said that he needed to spend and spend big. Ridsdale agreed, telling his manager that he would basically have an open cheque book that would come with one small condition- make sure that Leeds qualify for the Champions League again. It seemed like a simple task, O'Leary had already done it once and with a few more quality acquisitions he could surely do it again. Enter Robbie Fowler for 11 million GBP, Robbie Keane for 12 million GBP, Rio Ferdinand for 18 million GBP and Seth Johnson for 7 million GBP. The fact that O'Leary spent 7 million on Seth Johnson may be reason enough for him to be in this list, but add that to the fact that even with this star studded group of players that also included the likes of Harry Kewell and Mark Viduka, Leeds basically threw away a Champions League spot in 2002 as they slipped from top spot on 1st January, to 5th by the end of the season. The slide basically cemented their downfall as the whole of the club's budget was based around Champions League Football. Chairman Peter Ridsdale had put his faith in a manager, and after spending around 100 million GBP that manager had failed to deliver. That is why David O'Leary makes my list of the premiership's worst ever managers, and that is why O'Leary should never be trusted by any chairman ever again.

Christian Gross

CHRISTIAN GROSS IS LIKE THE ALEX FERGUSON of Swiss football. His amazing record in his home country includes six league championships, two with Grasshoppers of Zurich and four with FC Basel, as well as five Swiss cups and a couple of great runs in the European Champions League. But when he tried to ply his trade in the English Premiership his seeming tactical genius tended to get lost in translation.

He didn't help himself when he turned up late to his very own unveiling, flapping a ticket to the London underground, saying, "I want this to become my ticket to the dreams." Murdering the English language became the Gross trade mark giving the English press an easy target, which wasn't helped when Spurs got thumped 6-1 by Chelsea in just his second game in charge. After nine months and signing the likes of Nicola Berti, Frode Grodas and Paolo Tramezzani, Chairman Alan Sugar decided that his Swiss experiment had failed and Gross was given the boot. The Spurs fans can now look back on the Gross era and laugh along with the rest of the world. But for the man himself his tough times in England are nothing to laugh at, as he feels he was not given the respect he deserved during his time, all the while suffering at the hands of lazy players.

"You can never say never in football, but you must agree that the story certainly seems over for me in England," said Gross as he remembered his time as Spurs manager in an interview with *The Telegraph* Newspaper. "The way I am remembered there would make it very difficult for me to ever go back. But people forget I took over that club when they only had 13 points from 15 games. So it was never going to be easy." He went on to blame the laziness of the players for the club's poor performance during his reign, saying, "The biggest mistake I ever made at Tottenham was to replace Espen Baardsen in goal with Ian Walker. I picked Baardsen when Walker was injured for a while, but putting him back in the first team is something I really do regret. He is not a winner and never will be. He was lazy."

A poor tradesman always blames his tools. Christian, you were crap. Now just get over it.

Mick McCarthy

JUST 15 POINTS IN THE 2005-2006 SEASON WITH Sunderland says it all, really.

Les Reed

LES REED HONED HIS FOOTBALLING THEORY PLAYING in the reserves for the likes of Cambridge, Watford and Wycombe Wanderers before coaching Woodford Town to promotion from some obscure Pub League. He then went through a number of different jobs with the FA, before Alan Curbishley took him on as his assistant at Charlton Athletic. While there is no doubt that the guy obviously has some abilities as a coach, you only have to look at the likes of Brian Kidd and Sammy Lee to see that good coaches don't always make good managers. That point was underlined when Reed was thrown in at the deep end after

Ian Dowie was sacked as Charlton boss in November 2006. Les Reed lasted just six weeks in charge; six weeks that included just one win and a Carling Cup exit to Wycombe Wanderers. Reed was so bad that even during his short spell he gained the nickname 'Les Misarables' from the British press.

Mistaken Identity

EVERYONE REMEMBERS THE 1986 WORLD CUP QUARTER final between Argentina and England for just two things: Maradona's cheating hand of God, and his wonder goal just five minutes later. But the game also saw the emergence of a superb English talent that very nearly changed the course of football history on that sunny day in Mexico. If it hadn't been for a loud mouthed commentator by the name of Barry Davies, we would probably be calling John Barnes 'Sir' and bowing down at the feet of his bronze statue sat outside Wembley stadium

It was late in the second half and England was chasing the game. Maradona had been simply magnificent all day, conducting his team like an orchestra from the middle of the field and giving the England players a pure football lesson. They needed something special to get back into the game, something that the Argentineans wouldn't be expecting. England boss, Bobby Robson, decided that now was the right time to unleash John Barnes. Up until then Barnes had been nothing but a bit part player for England. Despite his scintillating performances at club level for Watford where he showed devastating pace, skill and crossing ability he was finding it difficult to dislodge the more senior players of the England side. But the time for John Barnes had come as Robson brought him on in place of Trevor Steven in the 74th minute. His impact on the game was immediate as the

Argentinean defenders struggled to contain his runs down the left. In the 80th minute his persistence paid off. Barnes shifted the ball on to his left boot and whipped in an early cross that seemed to catch everyone by surprise. Well, everyone except the competition's top goal scorer, Gary Lineker, who nodded the ball into the net from close range. England was not only back in it, they were in control and just a few minutes later the Lineker-Barnes combination was again in full effect. Again, it was Barnes that picked out the England striker with a superb cross. It looked certain that Lineker would equalize. So certain in fact that commentator, Barry Davies, screamed "GOAL" before the ball had even reached Lineker's head, putting poor Gary off the job at hand and his header hit the post. To this day I feel that the man who once famously but very stupidly said, "If that had gone in, it would have been a goal," jinxed us out of one of the most amazing comebacks in World Cup history. But despite the stupidity of Mr. Davies a new England star had been born, and the whole world would now know the name, John Barnes.

While the rest of the world, and indeed England, may have only just caught on and realized how good Barnsey really was, within football circles his skills were no secret. Three years earlier, at just 20 years of age, John Barnes broke into the Watford first team and formed a devastating strike partnership with Luther Blissett. With Barnes's pace and vision alongside the hustle and bustle style of Blissett, Watford went on to finish 2nd in the old English first division behind Liverpool, which is still their highest ever league finish. The performances of the front two were starting to attract some interest from abroad, with Italian giants AC Milan leading the way. After a few scouting missions to Vicarage Road, the Milan board decided that the abilities of John Barnes would be better suited to Serie A, and went about putting together a deal to sign the youngster. But one day, in the summer of 1983, it was Luther Blissett who found himself in the black and red striped shirt of Milan, playing in front of thousands of passionate Italians at the famous San Siro stadium, after an amazing 1 million GBP move. The move seemed to shock everyone in football, even the Watford faithful who saw it as a bitter sweet move. On one hand they were losing a hero, on the other, someone was stupid enough to pay 1 million for Blissett.

After five goals in 30 appearances Blissett's time in Italy can hardly be seen as successful, and after just one year away he was sold back to Watford for 550,000 GBP, which is just over half of what the Italians had paid for him in the first place. So you have to wonder, what caused the turn around? What was it that saw Blissett playing in Italy instead of the younger, more exciting, prospect of John Barnes?

The very politically incorrect version of events goes something like this. After hearing reports coming out of England that Watford had an exciting prospect, AC Milan sent scouts over to see what all the fuss was about. The scout returned to Milan with glowing reports and at the end of the 1982 – 83 season, a representative was sent over to England with very simple but pretty vague instructions that he must "sign the black guy that plays upfront for Watford." When the representative arrived at Vicarage Road he found that he was spoiled for choice as there were in fact two black guys playing for Watford. But rather than contacting his bosses back in Milan the representative either decided to use his own initiative, or he took the advice of Graeme Souness, and went about signing Watford's top goal scorer, Luther Blissett.

No one from Milan has ever admitted to the blunder. In fact, the general perspective in Italy is that they were after a big, bumbling striker to lead the line.

"Even the most ignorant and provincial person could see that Blissett and Barnes looked absolutely nothing alike. Second, the fact is that at that time Milan were looking for an out-and-out goal scorer and Barnes just wasn't that type of player," said well known journalist Gabriele Marcotti talking about the incident during an interview with Britain's *Guardian* newspaper in 2005.

And if you take into account his hat-trick for England against Luxembourg in only his second appearance, his golden boot award at the end of the 1982 - 83 season, (Yes, believe it or not Luther Blissett was awarded the European golden boot award for scoring more league goals than any other player in Europe, with 27,) and seven preseason goals for new club AC Milan, you can see how the Italians could have been duped by a man who was just going through something of a purple patch. But whether they wanted to sign Blissett or not, his purple patch came to an abrupt end and the Rossenari were left with egg on their faces. Luther Missit, as he was becoming affectionately known, failed to score in his next 12 international outings and even saw a penalty kick bounce back off row Z in the San Siro. His signing even saw the downfall of Milan's former owner who eventually went bankrupt and was forced to go into hiding. But Milan fans now look back on the Luther Blissett era with fond, comic nostalgia, the same way Liverpool fans might see Istvan Kozma, Spurs fans Ramon Vega, Evertonian Billy Kenny, and Gooner's fans Gus Ceasar. Well done, Luther.

What If?

JOHN BARNES COMPLETED HIS 1 MILLION GBP MOVE from Watford to AC Milan on 24th July 1983. His move came as a bit of a surprise to many in the football world, but not to Barnes's former manager who said this about losing the emerging talent, "John, without doubt, has the potential to be the best player in the world."

Barnes made his full Milan debut after a string of positive reserve team games against Juventus and became an instant hit with the fans at the San Siro. With his relaxed style of play, quick feet, great vision and flair, he reminded his adoring Italian fans more of a Brazilian than the boring English players they had seen in Serie A before. In just his second season at the club he was awarded the Serie A Player of The Year award and was hailed as "Il nuovo Pele" or "The New Pele" by the Italian press. But despite his phenomenal form for Milan, England boss, Bobby Robson, seemed reluctant to give him a real opportunity at international level.

In the summer of 1986 Barnes was named in the England squad to travel to Mexico for the upcoming World Cup, but was once again left on the bench for the opening game. England cruised through to the Quarter finals stage, but pressure from the English tabloids was building on Robson to include Barnes in the team to add some pace and skill out wide. On 22nd June he finally crumbled, and John Barnes was named in the starting line up to face Argentina.

The first half of this mammoth quarter final clash was tight and finished 0-0 with both teams looking tense. Barnes looked good out wide for England and Maradona was beginning to produce his best form for Argentina in the middle of the park, but it wasn't until early in the second half that the breakthrough came. Maradona had chased a long hopeful ball in behind the English defence. He jumped to challenge goalkeeper Peter Shilton. The ball seemed to evade them both and trickled into the back of the net. Shilton was livid, complaining that Maradona had handled the ball. But his argument fell on deaf ears and the goal stood.

From the kick off, Barnes picked up the ball and ran hard at the Argentina defence. He skinned Jose Cuciuffo on the edge of the box and drilled a low shot past Nery Pumpido in the Argentine goal for the equalizer. The goal is one of the greatest in the history of English football and caused a piece commentary that would be quoted for years to come by fans all around the world from commentator Barry Davies:

RUN AT HIM. BLOODY RUN AT HIM, BARNSEY. YEEEEEEAAAHHHHHHH, HE DID IT. THE BASTARD DID IT. I TOLD YOU, ROBBO. I TOLD YOU TO PLAY HIM. YOU CAN STICK YOUR MARADONA UP YOUR ARSE, BECAUSE THAT IS QUITE SIMPLY THE GREATEST GOAL YOU WILL EVER SEE.

From here, England were always on top. Barnes had the measure of man marker Jose Brown and later on he turned the tired Argentine defender inside out, creating two late goals for England striker, Gary Lineker, to seal a 3-1 victory. The performance put Barnes on the top of world football, but it was his two goals in the final against Germany that clinched England their second World Cup win and saw the man cement his place as one of the legends of the game.

So popular was he in his home country that when the new Wembley stadium was built in 2006 a bronze statue was erected outside to match the one already at Milan's San Siro stadium in honour of the great man.

Madness or Genius

IF ANY STORY DEMONSTRATES THE THEORY THAT the line between madness and genius is a very fine one, it is that of Eric Cantona. No one disputes that Cantona was a talented footballer. He was blessed with two great feet, great vision and an ability to read the game that can only be attributed to a handful of players throughout the history of the game. But on more than one occasion his abilities were over shadowed by a self destructive temper that exploded far too regularly and even cut short his international career.

Eric Cantona burst onto the French football scene in 1983, at the age of just 17, playing for Auxerre. His first foray into top flight football was cut short when, just a year after his impressive debut, after he was called up to complete his national service. He resigned for Auxerre in 1986 and was soon demonstrating that he had something very, very special. He was hailed as the future of French football by the press, and even picked up French legend Michel Platini as his number one fan. But in 1987 Cantona began to show signs of an aggressive streak that could ruin his career.

A training ground argument resulted in Cantona giving goal keeper Bruno Martini a smack in the face. Cantona was fined for the incident but it was by no means the end of his indiscretions. Eric was still producing the goods on the field though, helping the French under 21s win the European

Championships in 1988, but despite his obvious ability, Auxerre were becoming tired of the young Cantona's constant outbursts, and after he was banned for two games because of a dangerous tackle on Nantes player, Michel Der Zakarian, he was sold to Marseille for a French record 2.3 million GBP.

The move should have been a dream come true for Cantona as he had been a long time supporter of the club, but he failed to settle and his frustrations soon began to surface. They all came to a head after he was substituted during a friendly match with Torpedo Moscow. Cantona had been struggling to get a grip on the game and was taking constant abuse from the Moscow fans. The Marseille coach, Gérard Gili, decided to pull Eric from the pitch before he did anything stupid. But it was that decision that pushed Cantona over the edge and, after kicking the ball at the Moscow fans, he ripped off his shirt and threw it to the ground. Cantona was banned for one month and then quickly loaned out to Bordeaux where he seemed to regain focus on his football, wowing fans by scoring 6 goals in 11 games. From there he was sent on a year long loan to Montpellier. It was here that Cantona got himself into another highly publicized fight, throwing his boots at the face of team mate Jean-Claude Lemoult. Fans, press and players called for his resignation, but Cantona's immense skills were not lost on some of the Montpellier squad including Columbian, Carlos Valderrama, and fellow Frenchman, Laurant Blanc. They persuaded the club that Cantona had stupendous talent and that they couldn't expect any type of success without him in the team. The board fell for it and instead of being sacked, Cantona received a ten day ban and went on to help Montpellier lift the French Cup.

After returning to Marseille, Cantona's form once again slipped, mainly due to injury, and the French side decided to cut their losses by selling him to Nimes. But Cantona was becoming very disillusioned with the game he loved and was already considering an early retirement when he once again exploded. During a match Cantona lost his temper with a referee after he made a dubious decision. Cantona seemed to take it personally and, when shrugging his shoulders in the smug Gallic way that became his trade mark in his future career at Manchester Utd, didn't seem to be cutting the mustard, he picked up the ball instead and threw it at the official. Because this wasn't his first indiscretion, Cantona was called before the French Football Federation for a disciplinary hearing. After handing Cantona a one month ban, the head of the Federation said, "You can't be judged like any other player. Behind you there is a trail of the smell of sulphur. You can't expect anything from an individualist like you." Cantona obviously didn't agree with the statement or the sentence handed out and he subsequently walked up to every member of the committee calling each of them an "idiot". The ban was increased to three months and he announced his retirement soon after.

Michel Platini, who had been a long time fan of Cantona, decided that he wasn't going to let this talent go to waste and made it his goal to rebuild the troubled star's career. Platini recommended that Cantona see a psychoanalyst who proposed that a change of scenery could be the key to resurrecting his passion. "He told me I should consider moving to England," said Cantona looking back on a troubled time in his career. The future French National Coach, Gerard Houllier agreed that a move to England away from the French press could be just the thing to bring Cantona's attention back to his passion for football, and Platini then went about making hasty plans for the move. On the sixth of November 1991 Auxerre were playing against Liverpool at Anfield in the second leg of their UEFA cup tie. The French side had taken a 2-0 lead in to the game from the first leg, but Liverpool pulled out an amazing performance to win the game 3-0 and progress to the next round 3-2 on aggregate. After the game, Platini approached Liverpool's Graeme Souness with an offer that he thought was impossible to refuse. He told Souness that Eric Cantona was looking for a move to England and that his first choice was the famous Liverpool FC. But it seems that Cantona's fiery reputation had already spread across the English Channel, and Souness made one of those amazingly astute tactical decisions that would bring him so much success in the future, (ha), and politely declined the offer stating that he would be concerned about the dressing room harmony with Cantona at the club. Souness signed Nigel Clough two years later for 2.5 Million GBP instead. Nice one, Graeme.

In fact, Platini struggled to find any club to take on his protégé, but Sheffield Wednesday agreed to give him a one week trial. Wednesday manager, Trevor Francis, and the Hillsborough board all found the Frenchman extremely polite and thought that his wild days were well and truly behind him. But after a practice match was cancelled due to bad weather Francis took a leaf out of the coaching book of Graeme Souness and, despite being impressed by Cantona's work in training, refused to offer him a contract until he had seen him play in a proper match. Cantona signed for Leeds Utd just one week later. Despite scoring nine goals in 28 very impressive performances, a league champions medal and no temper tantrums, Leeds Manager, Howard Wilkinson, decided to sell him for a bargain 1.25 million GBP to rivals Manchester Utd. He thought that he would also be getting Utd defender Dennis Irwin in return. But the Irishman failed to agree to terms and Wilkinson was left empty handed. From here on, Cantona simply became known as "King Eric" on the terraces at Old Trafford, and even after he karate kicked a fan during a match at Selhurst

Park, waffled on about seagulls and trailers before telling *Four Four Two* magazine that he should have hit the fan harder, he has managed to cement himself as a legend of the game.

What If?

AFTER FRENCHMAN ERIC CANTONA COMPLETED A WEEK'S trial at English club Sheffield Wednesday, Wednesday Manager, Trevor Francis, still wasn't 100% convinced that the player was ready to play in the Premier League, but was ready to offer him a week's extension to the trial. Cantona scoffed at the idea and was ready to try his luck elsewhere when Sheffield Wednesday's star forward, David Hirst, heard that his boss was stalling over the deal and pulled him aside one morning. Hirst felt that Cantona would be a superb acquisition and actually threatened to hand in a transfer request if Francis didn't sign him to the club. Eric Cantona signed a one year deal with Sheffield Wednesday on the 23rd of January 1992 and made his debut against Luton Town on 1st of February. The match could have been sold out twice over as the Hillsborough faithful were desperate to catch a glimpse of the flamboyant Frenchman that could just be the missing link in their title challenge. Cantona started the game on the bench and was brought on with just 15 minutes to go, giving him little chance to impress. Despite this and the fact that he was stuck out wide on the right, Eric showed enough clever touches to become an instant hit with the fans. Over the next few weeks, Wednesday Manager, Trevor Francis, refrained from naming Cantona in his starting line-up much to the annoyance of the Wednesday faithful who were beginning to bombard local radio stations and newspapers with complaints about the way Francis was handling the new star. Francis finally caved in to the pressure and gave Cantona his first real chance to impress on 7th March at home against Coventry City. Cantona was once again played wide right and had little effect in a boring first half Wednesday display. Cantona came out for the second half looking like a different player. He started to get involved more, linking up with the front two and drifting inside with devastating effect. In the 56th minute John Harkes picked up the ball on the left and ghosted inside. As he looked up, he noticed Cantona making a diagonal run from right to left and played a beautiful reverse pass right in to his path. Cantona took one touch, looked up and crossed the ball with his left boot right on to the head of David Hirst, who somehow, from just eight yards out, hit the up right. The ball bounced away and after a quick counter attack, Coventry City forward, Peter Ndlovu, slid the ball into the back of the net to give his side the lead. Just two minutes later Eric Cantona's number went up on the side of the pitch as Trevor Francis looked to make some changes, but the Frenchman refused to leave the field. The Hillsborough crowd booed and hissed at the decision of their manager who had now been asked by the referee to get Cantona off the pitch before the game could continue. Francis walked over to Eric to explain that his day's work was finished, but Cantona pushed his boss to the floor and climbed into the crowd, disappearing amongst the mass of blue and white striped shirts.

After the game Francis stated that Cantona's contract would be, "cancelled with immediate effect," and that he had made the decision to pull Cantona from the game because, "he had failed in his positional and defensive duties that led to the Coventry goal." Cantona replied to the statement a few weeks later from his home in France by saying, "Trevor Francis has got the tactical knowledge of a gold fish," and that he would be of better use, "cleaning the

Hillsborough toilets."

The whole debacle had a negative effect on the Sheffield team as they ended the season in 6th place after a promising start. Trevor Francis was sacked in June 1992.

Cantona instantly became a recluse. Disillusioned by all in the football world, he locked himself away and piled on the weight. Late in 1993 Cantona's mentor, Michel Platini, paid him a visit in the hope that he could pull him out of what was now a deep depression. After a long talk with the French legend, Cantona decided that enough was enough and went back into training. But at the start of the 1994-95 season Cantona still hadn't found himself a club as no one was willing to take a risk on such a volatile talent.

After doing the rounds of nearly 20 different clubs Eric Cantona finally found a home at English first division side, Tranmere Rovers, whom he signed for on 28th August 1994. In his first season he was absolutely sensational playing alongside former Liverpool player John Aldridge. Cantona scored 25 goals league goals in a partnership that amassed 61 and helped the club achieve promotion to the Premier League. It wasn't long before the so called glamour clubs were once again sniffing around with Manchester Utd manager, Sir Alex Ferguson, trying on several occasions to get Cantona to Old Trafford, but even though he had a 5 million GBP bid accepted by Tranmere, Cantona refused the move saying that Rover manager John King was "the greatest in the world" and that he would "never play for anyone else." Cantona retired at the end of the 1996-97 after helping Tranmere to 8th in the Premiership, which was their highest ever league finish.

Welcome to Hell

UNLIKE THE MAJORITY OF BRAZILIAN FOOTBALLERS, Ricardo Izecson dos Santos Leite, or Kaka as he is more commonly known, had a childhood that was relatively free of money troubles. His father was an engineer and could afford to give his son a good education at a school in Sao Paulo. But despite his comfortable upbringing Kaka had the same dream as almost every other young boy in Brazil- to become a professional football player. The difference between Kaka and all the other children was that he had an unbelievable natural ability, and at the tender age of eight he was picked up by one of the giants of Brazilian football, and his home town club, Sao Paulo, after playing in a local tournament.

The rise and rise of Kaka nearly ended when he was just 18 after a swimming pool accident nearly paralysed him from the neck down. Just his recovery from such an injury is amazing. The fact that he is playing football at such a high level is simply a miracle, and one that he puts down to God.

"I was sliding into this swimming pool but fell awkwardly and hit my head on the bottom of the pool," he said in an interview with Britain's *Sun* newspaper. "I twisted my neck but did not realise at the time that I had broken my sixth cervical bone. I went back to my club, Sao Paulo, the following day and actually trained for a couple of days. But I was in such pain that the club eventually sent me to hospital for tests. The doctor was trying not to frighten me but admitted I was very lucky to have been able to train for two days with a broken neck and not suffer permanent damage. All I knew as a kid was that anyone with a broken neck would be disabled for life so my immediate question was: Would I ever be able to play football again? The doctor told me I would not be able to play for at least three months and I would have to wear a cervical collar all that time. Then they would be able to tell if I was going to fully recover. But after two months, the injury had healed and I was able to resume my football career. That was when I knew God was looking after me and that He was on my side."

After the 2007 Champions League win over Liverpool, Kaka confirmed his all encompassing faith when he revealed a t-shirt that said, "I belong to Jesus" when he collapsed on the floor. Kaka also calls himself, "God's own player."

The injury did nothing to halt the young superstar's progress as nearly every club in Europe was lined up to sign the latest wonder kid from Brazil. But Kaka resisted the urge to move abroad too early, and his patience paid off in 2003 when he joined AC Milan in Italy for 5 million GBP. During his time at Milan, Kaka quickly became one of the hottest properties in world football, helping his new side to the Serie A title in 2004 and their seventh European title in 2007 before a record breaking 56 million GBP move to Real Madrid in 2009.

But Kaka's career nearly took a strange twist very early on. It was a few months before the injury that nearly crippled the promising young Brazilian. His reputation was starting to spread to Europe and a number of clubs were looking to give him his opportunity with a cash strapped Sao Paolo looking to cash in. It wasn't Europe's elite that was trying to coax him away from his home land and moves to lesser clubs in France, Germany and England were apparently talked about. But it was Gaziantepspor in Turkey that were the only club to make a formal offer. Although their first bid was rejected by Sao Paulo the small Turkish club were told that they could have him if they were willing to increase their initial bid to around 1.5 million GBP. Looking back on what the man has gone on to achieve you would have to say that 1.5 million GBP is a bloody bargain, but at the time Kaka had hardly made a dent in first team football and there was no guarantee that his sparkling performances in the Brazilian youth sides would continue. So the Turks considered the fee to be too high and passed up the opportunity to sign one of the greatest players of his generation. DOH!

What If?

18 YEAR OLD BRAZILIAN WONDER KID, KAKA, SIGNED for little known Turkish club, Gaziantepspor, for 1.5 million GBP on the 5th of June 2000. The move came as something of surprise to many in the football world as Kaka was considered to be the next big thing and was being scouted by the likes of Juventus, Real Madrid and Manchester Utd, but with Sao Paulo short of cash and with no other solid bids coming through, the Brazilian club cashed in.

Whether the move was the right one for such an exciting prospect didn't matter as he pulled on his Gaziantepspor shirt for the first time against the giants of Turkish giants Galatasaray. Galatasaray fans are well known for their passion, often displaying banners saying "Welcome to hell," to intimidate opposing players. On this occasion they were in full voice. Flairs, noise and smoke filled the stadium as the two sides were led on to the pitch. Far from being nervous, Gaziantepspor's latest signing was used to such atmospheres from his time in Brazil, and was simply thriving under the pressure, desperate to get out on the pitch and show his stuff. After five minutes Kaka picked up the ball out on the right just inside his own half. He side stepped Hakan Unsal, flicked the ball past Carlos Carpone, showed him a clean pair of heels and cracked a right foot shot that flicked off the top of the crossbar. The crowd inside the Ali Sami Yen Stadium became a little quieter and when a deft Kaka flick set up the first goal you could have heard a pin drop. Early in the second half Kaka was at it again. He did a clever step over, leaving Gheorghe Hagi on the deck before forcing a great save from goal keeper Karem Inan. It was obvious that the Galatasaray defence simply couldn't cope and in the 70th minute they decided to do something about it. The ball fell at Kaka's feet on the edge of the area and before he had time to think, Gheorghe Popescu, slid in with a crunching tackle leaving the young Brazilian stricken on the floor. The Gaziantepspor bench and the few fans packed into a corner of the stadium were furious, shouting obscenities and invading the pitch. Kaka had already got back to his feet and seemed to be ok, but that did nothing to curb rising tension between the two sets of fans.

In the 81st minute Gaziantepspor were once again on the attack. The players were still totally unaware of the fights that were now breaking out all over the ground. And when the ball fell at the feet of Kaka for him to roll the ball into the empty net giving his team a 2-0 lead those fights spilled on to the pitch. The referee and his assistants instantly signalled for the players to return to their dressing rooms, but before he could get there Kaka was set upon by a group of Galatasaray fans. They kicked, punched and even stabbed him in the leg with a screwdriver and it took a number of police as well as several Gaziantespor players to get Kaka free and back into the stadium. It was reported that the young Brazilian was unconscious for around 10 minutes, suffered a fractured cheekbone, two broken ribs and needed a total of 25 stitches. His injured cheek bone required several surgeries, meaning that he would be missing from football for up to three months.

During his enforced break from the game the rumours surrounding Kaka's future were all over the news. Would he quit the game after his horrific ordeal? Would he go home to Brazil? Or would he try his luck with another club in Europe? But what he did next shocked the whole world. Kaka refused to press charges against his attackers and pledged to help them through any rehabilitation that they may need. He also decided to stay on in Turkey for at least the remainder of his contract, rejecting a very lucrative offer to return home. Kaka put his surprise decisions down to his massive faith in God.

"God has been watching over me and protected me from two injuries that could have ended my career," he said in an interview with an Italian radio station. "I am here because God has given me work to do and I will stay here until I feel that God is telling me to move on."

Kaka stayed in Turkey for five years, guiding the small club to an amazing run of success that included three league titles and a Champions League semi final appearance. In another shock move, Kaka turned down the opportunity to play for Real Madrid. Instead, he moved to London signing for Tottenham Hotspur for a measly 3 million GBP. You wish, Hibberd.

Bloody Work Permits and Being Outbid By Manchester Utd

SOMETIMES YOU DO THE SCOUTING, GET THE MONEY OFF the chairman and verbally agree terms with the player—only for the transfer gods to poke you in the eye and tell you that he can't have a work permit, or for Manchester Utd to come from out of the depths and outbid you by about 5 million, making all of your original hard work worthless. It can be very frustrating, especially being an Arsenal fan and seeing how being spat on by the transfer market red tape or getting outbid by rival clubs can make you miss out on some of the greatest players in the history of the game.

There is no doubt that under manager, Arsene Wenger, Arsenal has developed one of the best scouting systems in the world. Wenger relies on his abilities to spot up and coming talent so that he can sign them for nominal fees before turning them into world beaters. Adebayour, Ashley Cole and Theo Walcott have all come from this amazing Arsenal production line that looks like it will simply never end. But producing and spotting such talent can be a hard, laborious job. Sometimes you can search and search, watch game after game and video after video and be offered nothing but a bunch of Ade Akinbyis or Jason "Pineapple

68

Head" Lees. On other occasions, players can simply jump up and smack you in the face saying, "Sign me you dopey bastard," and in 2002 that is exactly what happened for Arsenal. At the time the Arsenal scouting system was spreading its tentacles all over Europe looking for one of those special talents of the world game when, during a routine scouting mission to Spain to watch the Barcelona youth side, something amazing happened.

There were two players in particular that stood out head and shoulders above the rest, two players that Arsene Wenger decided instantly that he wanted to sign. The first was a 15 year old Spanish Midfielder by the name of Cesc Fabregas. Arsenal were surprised when the Catalan club decided to let Fabregas go so easily. His silky skills, passing ability and amazing goal scoring record from midfield in the Barca youth team, had seen him become something of a legend around the club. But Barcelona's loss was definitely Arsenal's gain, and since they signed him in September 2003 he has gone on to become the club's youngest ever player, goal scorer, captain and one of the most wanted players in the world.

While the signing of Fabregas has been a great moment in the history of Arsenal Football Club there was another player in that Barcelona youth team that nearly made the move to Highbury, a player who, if he had signed with Fabregas would surely have guided Arsenal to a lot more success than they have managed over the last few years. That player was none other than Argentine superstar Diego Maradona's heir apparent, Lionel Messi. Arsenal were desperate to sign the youngster along with Cesc Fabregas, and for Messi the move seemed to be a positive one as it would bring with it the promise of first team football. But while the transfer gods were more than happy to let Arsenal have one up and coming world beater, there was no way that they were going to be allowed to have two, and

Messi's move to the Gooners was soon lost in the red tape of the dreaded work permit.

"He was in the same team as Cesc Fabregas, but we couldn't do anything because he is Argentine and that causes work permit problems," said chief scout Steve Rowley in an interview with Britain's *Daily Mail* newspaper.

But the bad luck for Arsenal didn't end there as another wonder kid was also destined to play his football elsewhere. In 2003, just as Fabregas was completing his move to Arsenal and the disappointment of missing out on Messi was beginning to pass, Arsene Wenger was over in Portugal trying his best to woo the mother of another potential superstar, Cristiano Ronaldo.

"After I signed for Manchester United, she and I were sitting watching a Premier League game on television," said Ronaldo, "and she yelled out, 'I know that guy. I liked him.' "

Wenger had succeeded in winning over the player's mother, but despite three personal meetings with the player and presenting him with an Arsenal shirt that already had his name on the back, it seemed that Ronaldo's future had already been mapped out for him.

"I had Ronaldo at the training ground," said Wenger in a recent press conference. "I showed him around and I gave him a shirt. It had got his name on the back. But in the end it was a question of the amount of transfer fee between the two clubs. Of course, he has proved to be a bargain (at 12.25 million GBP). But the price that we discussed was, in fact, much lower; it was divided by three. What killed the deal was that United came back from the States and played against Sporting Lisbon, and Ronaldo was man of the match. The United players must have been dead coming out of the plane and Ronaldo was fresh, so he must have been even more dominant. United had a partnership agreement with Lisbon, and in that partnership they played them after coming back from the States. There was also Carlos Queiroz (United's Portuguese former assistant manager). He knew Ronaldo well and since then United have signed Anderson and Nani from Portugal as well because of Carlos Queiroz. It's like I can sign players from France because I know them well."

But in the end Ronaldo will definitely go down as "The one that got away," in the eyes of Arsene Wenger. Something that he summed up in an interview with *The Guardian* by saying "I'm disappointed that I seduced only Ronaldo's mum."

Oh, well, Mr Arsene, you can't win them all.

What If?

WHAT IF ARSENAL HAD RONALDO, LIONEL MESSI and Cesc Fabregas playing for them? It is quite simple, really.

Premier League Champions
2004-2005 Arsenal
2005-2006 Arsenal
2006-2007 Arsenal
2007-2008 Arsenal
2008-2009 Arsenal

Well, that is if Mr Wenger didn't sell them all on for a healthy profit after just one year, of course.

Toffee Headache

SUPPORTING EVERTON CAN BE VERY FRUSTRATING AT TIMES. For their diehard fans it must be similar to riding a very big and very scary roller coaster (Please excuse the horrible cliché) as they have gone from dominating the league in the mid 80s and challenging in Europe, to battling relegation throughout the 90s, narrowly avoiding the drop on the final day, twice. The club has shown moments of revival, moments when they looked like once again reaching the pinnacle of English football, only to be shot back down by some very poor business decisions.

In 1994, Everton went in to the final game of the season against Wimbledon needing to win to keep their place in the Premier League. The first half the game didn't go well for the Everton faithful who had packed in to Goodison Park, expecting miracles. The team was looking shaky and extremely nervous right from the start, something that wasn't helped when Swedish international, Anders Limpar, handled the ball in the area that resulted in Dean Holdsworth slotting home a penalty to give Wimbledon an early lead. Then, just minutes later, Everton's 40 year top flight status looked well and truly over when defender, Gary Ablett, scored a shocking own goal. It would have been a terrible blow for the club that was already short of cash. They would have had to sell off some of their star players and it could have taken years for them to bounce back. But just before half time their hope was restored when Limpar was brought down in the box and Graham Stuart showed nerves of steel, having already missed one spot kick, to smash Everton back into the game. At half time it was 2-1 to Wimbledon.

At the same time, just two hours away in Birmingham, Everton's local rivals, Liverpool, were playing against Aston Villa. As news of Everton's predicament was announced over the loud speakers a party seemed to breakout amongst the Liverpool fans, and chants of "The shit are going down," rang out around Villa Park. It was looking like a good way for Liverpool to end the season as they were also leading through a Robbie Fowler goal.

It seemed that Everton and their new Manager, Mike Walker, would need God himself to come down and intervene if they were to get out of this one. Or at the very least Walker would have to produce a stirring and motivating speech that even Winston Churchill would have been proud of. But, if anything, going in at half time 2-1 down and being almost certain of relegation was probably the best thing that could have happened to them. They were down, they were out and what the fuck did they have left to lose?

When the second half kicked off it was instantly obvious that whatever had happened in the Everton dressing room had worked. Whether they had all been snorting Columbian marching powder, injecting steroids, reading the Bible or just sitting in silence looking at Mike Walker thinking, *'It's your fucking fault we are in this predicament,'* the nerves were gone and they began playing with a fearless attacking attitude that was causing the Wimbledon defence all sorts of problems. As the game continued, it also seemed that luck was on their side as John Ebbrell stopped an almost certain goal by clearing a Marcus Gayle header off the line and Graham Stuart was lucky not to concede a penalty when he seemed to handle the ball in the area. Then, just for one moment, it seemed that God had indeed come to Everton's aid when he inhabited the body of Barry Horne who strode through Wimbledon midfield like a gazelle. Horne looked smooth, skilful and Maradona-like as he cracked a shot from thirty yards that struck the underside of the bar and bounced into the net. Well, either that or the big guy stumbled through a couple of challenges, lost his bearings, then closed his eyes and took a wild swing at the ball. But whatever the circumstances, it was his first goal of the season and it brought Everton level. There was now an overwhelming air of belief floating around the ground. A draw was not good enough, but there was still plenty of time, Everton was now totally on top and it was surely only a matter of time before they snatched a winner.

With just ten minutes remaining, Everton midfielder Graham Stuart hit a daisy cutter from the edge of the area that somehow trickled past Hans Segers. The crowd went absolutely spastic because Everton, it seemed, had achieved the impossible. They had pulled off the ultimate Houdini and kept their place in England's Premier League. To top off a great day for the fans packed inside the stadium, Aston Villa had also pulled off a great comeback of their own to beat Liverpool 2-1. Not that any Evertonian really gave a shit what Liverpool was up to at that moment in time.

A few years later there was a lot of controversy surrounding the game against Wimbledon. Match fixing had raised its ugly head with Wimbledon goalkeeper Hans Segers being one of the players investigated. Up for scrutiny was his seemingly lazy effort to stop Graham Stuart's weak shot that led to Everton's winning goal. Segers was later cleared of all allegations to do with the crime but the argument still continues; was Segers paid off to make sure Everton were not relegated? Whether he was or not doesn't really matter, because, on that day, Everton deserved their win and their place in England's top flight.

The win and the performance lifted the spirits of everyone around the club. So much so that when the 1994 - 95 season kicked off everybody expected that a return to the glory days of the 1980s was just around the corner. They were right but it wouldn't be under the current regime.

Everton had paid Norwich City a hefty compensation fee when they attracted manager Mike Walker to the club in January 1994. But his victory on the final day of the season against Wimbledon proved to be his only piece of glory in his short reign as manager. In the following season, Everton failed to win a game going into November and Walker was sacked just ten months after taking charge. He did leave something of a parting gift for the fans and former Everton player, Joe Royale, who was lined up as his replacement, when he secured the loan signing of Glasgow Rangers striker Duncan Ferguson. Ferguson made his debut on the same night that Joe Royale took charge of his first game. It was the 21st of November 1994 and the opponents were local rivals, Liverpool. I happened to be at the game and as a Liverpool fan I would prefer not to talk about it too much, but Everton won 2-0, Ferguson scored and Joe Royal officially started "The Dogs of War" style of play that would bring Everton so much success in the following years.

By the end of 2005, Royale and his Everton side had kicked, tackled and hacked their way off the bottom of the table to finish 15th in the league seven points above the drop zone, which was an amazing feat considering their dreadful start. Even more amazing than their league form was their FA Cup run that ended with them beating Manchester Utd 1-0 in the final.

The next season Everton proved to be one of the

hardest teams in the league to beat, and with new signings such as, Andrei Kanchelskis from Manchester Utd, they finished 6th in the league. Despite a failure to build on this initial success, Joe Royale still had the full backing of fans and players alike, and was seen as the only person who would be able to take the club forward. But the Everton board, with questionable businessman Peter Johnson as Chairman, decided that consolidating their position financially was more important than moving the club forward on the field. This meant that massive restrictions in the transfer budget would hinder the manager's plans. Joe Royale was used to working under such conditions and sent his scouts to all corners of the world to find the club some worthy talent.

It was approaching transfer deadline day of the 1996 – 97 season. Joe Royale had been excited by two players who had been spotted playing for Brann in Norway. He approached the Everton board for the money, which was thought to be around 500,000 GBP, only for them to tell him he was being crazy. The rejection was the last straw for Royale who thought that the signings of the two Norwegian youngsters would have been ideal. Deciding he could no longer work for the club he loved as long as Peter Johnson was in charge, he quit before the season was out.

The players in question were defender Claus Eftevaag and striker Tore Andre Flo. While missing out on Eftevaag would not have hurt the club a great deal, there is no doubt that Flo would have been an amazing asset to the team, and that he could have formed a devastating partnership with Scot Duncan Ferguson. Instead, Flo joined Chelsea for just 350,000 GBP, scoring 34 goals in 112 league games before moving to Glasgow Rangers for 12 million GBP.

Everton fans were left wondering what Royale could have achieved if he had been left to his own devices. What players would he have brought in? Could he have built on the success he was had previously achieved? And would Flo and Ferguson have pushed them back toward the top of the table.

What If?

EVERTON SIGNED PROMISING NORWEGIAN STRIKER, Tore Andre Flo, on transfer deadline day 1997. Manager Joe Royale had threatened to quit after Chairman Peter Johnson had at first refused to stump up the money. The pair came to an agreement with Royale dropping his bid to sign defender, Claus Eftevaag, as well. Despite missing out on one of his targets, Royale was delighted that Flo had decided to join him at Goodison Park despite offers from other more glamorous clubs.

Royale decided to keep his new signing under wraps until the last game of the season against Chelsea on 11th May 1997. Flo started the game up front alongside Duncan Ferguson, the player that many in the football press thought may be under pressure from the new boy.

Just ten minutes into the game, the new strike partnership showed some promising signs when a flick on from Ferguson was met with a bullet header from Flo that clipped the outside of the post. The chance lifted the spirits around Goodison Park, and seemed to inject Flo with an unnerving air of confidence. It was obvious that for such a tall kid heading wasn't his only attribute. He began showing some neat touches, clever passes and quick feet creating opportunities for others as well as himself. In the 37th minute the Everton pressure that had been building from early on, finally paid off when midfielder Gary Speed popped up on the edge of the area and drilled a shot into the bottom corner. From here, Chelsea were lucky to get in at half time without conceding any more, but it only took two minutes of the second half for that to change, and for Tore Andre Flo, to break his Everton duck.

Again, it was a long ball forward from Everton defender Craig Short that caused all of the problems. The Chelsea defence let it bounce, giving Duncan Ferguson a chance to muscle his way in and knock the ball into the path of Flo, who was totally unmarked about 12 yards from goal. Flo took one touch to steady himself, looked up and picked out the top right hand corner with ease. It was a phenomenal finish, something that would become something of a trade mark during his time at Everton.

The 2-0 win made sure that Everton finished the season on a high, and after the performance of their latest signing, the Everton fans also had high hopes for the next season. The board also saw the potential and when Royale came forward asking for a 10 million GBP transfer kitty for the summer, they duly obliged.

Everton went on to sign Brazilian superstar Juninho from relegated club Middlesbrough on 30th July 1997 for 9.75 million GBP. The Everton fans were truly ecstatic and when they went through pre season winning every game, the talk around the club was of winning a major trophy and a possible top four finish.

Almost every side goes into a new season with high hopes of being the shock success of the season, but when Everton smashed Crystal Palace 5-0 on 9th August 1997 they suddenly had the rest of the league talking as well. By Christmas they were in third position, seven points off the top, and were playing an attacking style of football that was attracting a lot of positive attention. Gone were the long balls from Craig Short toward the towering Duncan Ferguson, to be replaced by a quick passing style that was carving apart defences. Ferguson was also showing a new side to himself. He still used his massive frame and lots of hustle and bustle, but he was also linking well with Juninho and new strike partner, Tore Andre Flo. Everton finished in third place as the league's top goal scorers. Although they were defeated in the FA Cup final, 1-0 by Arsenal, they had qualified for Europe, done the double over Liverpool, and were looking at a bright future with Joe Royale leading the way.

But Everton had just one problem; Peter Johnson was still the chairman and at the end of the day, Johnson had grown up as a Liverpool fan, was purely a business man at heart and probably didn't have the best interests of Everton FC in mind. It was simply all about the money. So, when Real Madrid came in with a 35 million GBP bid for Flo, Ferguson and Juninho he just couldn't resist. Royale quit the moment he heard, and Everton fans camped outside the stadium insisting that Johnson hand over control immediately. Johnson tried to ease the pressure by promising that the full amount would be available for new manager Walter Smith to spend. But Smith only spent 3 million GBP that summer and was forced to pick up a few free transfers during the next season to help them continue their progress. But despite the manager's best efforts Everton were the shock relegation team of the 1998-99 season. Peter Johnson stepped down as Chairman in the summer but it would take Everton years to recover from his poor management.

Forgotten Players of the English Premier League

Billy Kenny

IT WAS IN 1992, DURING THE VERY FIRST MERSEYSIDE derby of the English Premier League era, that the world was introduced to the mercurial talents of a 19 year old by the name of Billy Kenny. The youngster already had a great reputation, but when he came into the battle royal that is Everton Vs Liverpool he wore his blue shirt with pride, showed no fear, and earned himself the man of the match award as well as a call up to the England U21 squad. He was quickly named as the "Goodison Gazza" after England legend Paul Gascoigne, and it seemed that there was nothing that he couldn't do. In a game against Wimbledon he was on the end of the usual dirty bastard tactics from Dons midfielder, Vinnie Jones, who was booked for his actions. But rather than shy away from the game, as most youngsters would, Kenny got back to his feet and crunched Vinnie back just five minutes later. The tackle shook poor Vinnie up and he left the young lad alone for the rest of the match. This tackle almost proved to be Billy Kenny's finest hour as he soon fell into some bad habits. Many talented footballers have been blown away by the celebrity status that their fame can suddenly bring them. For George

Best, Paul Gascoigne and Paul Merson, that status and the endless parties almost became more important than the football. But while these three ended up with significant drinking and gambling problems, Billy Kenny took the downfall of the talented football player one step further.

"Some mornings I got home at four or five, had a couple of lines of cocaine, slept for an hour and then went to training," he said. "Sometimes I could hardly see the ball. I was a joke."

The player, who many think had more natural talent than Steven Gerrard, was sacked by Everton having made only 22 appearances, then by Oldham after 4, and later by Barrow Town. Billy Kenny later moved to America to escape his demons where he completed a degree in business and continued a life away from football.

Nii Lamptey

WHILE BILLY KENNY HAS ONLY HIMSELF TO BLAME FOR a promising career cut short, the fall of Nii Lamptey can only be put down to great personal tragedy, racism, greed and selfishness.

It was in 1991 that the young Ghanaian broke onto the world scene with his four goals in the U17 World Championships. His brilliance not only helped Ghana to the title, but it also saw him receive the best player of the tournament award, ahead of Argentina's Juan Sebastian Veron, and Italy's Alessandro Del Piero. The hype surrounding the youngster was immense, especially after Brazilian legend, Pele, named him as his very own heir apparent.

Nii Lamptey had a very tough upbringing. Raised in a poor suburb of Ghana by an alcoholic father, Lamptey's only escape was football. He regularly skipped school to kick the ball around with his friends, which helped hone his skills as a potential superstar of the game, but also meant that he never really learnt to read. After his amazing performance in the 1991 World Championships agents and clubs were scrambling over themselves to sign him up. But Lamptey, with his lack of education, was just happy to be living the dream of every African youngster. He knew he was going to be a professional footballer and signed the first contract that came his way.

He began his pro career playing for Anderlecht in Belgium, becoming the youngest ever player in the Belgian top flight when he made his debut at just 16. From his first game it was obvious that the young lad had a lot of talent and he quickly became a firm fans favourite. In 1993, after three years in Belgium he was transferred to Dutch side PSV Eindhoven as a replacement for Brazilian Romario, who had moved to Spanish club, Barcelona. Here his progress continued and he scored 10 goals in 22 league games. But as the hype around the new Pele increased and clubs from all around the world began scrambling over themselves to sign him, the contract that he had signed as a youngster with his Italian agent came back and bit him in the arse.

A well known German agent later labeled the man who drew up Nii Lampteys contract as, "a shady character who held Lamptey's transfer rights like a slave owner held his slave".

Not understanding what he was signing, Lamptey had got himself in to an exclusive marketing contract that gave his agent authority to arrange transfers without the player's say so. It also stated that the greedy bastard was entitled to take 25% of any fee paid for Lamptey. It was because of this that a string of transfers that were not in the best interest of the player were lined up. There was now no way out for the Ghanaian international who was transferred to premier league clubs Aston Villa and Coventry, where he failed to impress before being shipped off to Venezia in Italy all within the space of three years. During a spell at German side SpVgg his team mates refused to sleep in the same room as him. It was a level of racism that he had never witnessed before, and one that only added to a growing depression.

Off the field too, his life was filled with tragedy. It was while playing with Union de Santa Fe in Argentina that Lamptey's third child, Diego, contracted a rare disease and died. It was a terrible ordeal that he never really recovered from and one that was further inflicted upon him some years later when his daughter, Lisa, also died soon after birth of the same disease. The Ghanaian government refused to let Lamptey bring either of the deceased children back to his home country, so he was forced to bury both abroad.

"I buried them both alone," he said. "I've been through hell."

Lamptey blames his amazing misfortune on the Juju men, witch doctors, who apparently cursed him during his very first international appearance for Ghana against Togo in 1991.

"It was there. I can't hide it. I was vomiting blood on the pitch. So it is there when people want your downfall. I know if it was me alone and people had left me to be the way God created me and wanted me to be, for sure I should have been playing for Madrid now."

Lamptey is now living back in Ghana as a farmer. He has reconciled with the father that beat him as a youngster and is trying his best to learn from the obstacles that life has thrown his way. Good Luck Nii.

Rob Jones

ROB JONES WAS TRULY A SENSATION AFTER HE SIGNED for Liverpool from Crewe on 4th October 1991. He was spotted purely by luck by the then Liverpool manager, Graeme Souness, who was actually scouting another player at the time. But Souness had been so impressed by his performance that not only did he quickly stump up 300,000 GBP for the player but he also threw him into the starting line up to face Manchester Utd just two days later. Rob Jones was just 19 years old, but he handled the situation and Utd winger Ryan Giggs superbly, with Giggs later saying that Jones was the best defender he had ever played against. By the end of the 1991-92 season, Jones had earned himself a call up to Graham Taylor's England squad, and looked to be heading to the European Championships in Sweden only to be struck down by his first set of injury problems. For the next four years he was seen as one of the best right backs in the league despite never really being fully fit. He managed to earn himself eight England caps, but quickly fell behind the ever dependable Gary Neville as the first choice. In 1996, at the age of just 25, Jones was told that he needed a six month break from the game to get over a severe case of shin splints and chronic back problems. Jones tried to make a comeback but after a stop start couple of years and three knee operations he retired from the game aged 27. He is still seen by most Liverpool fans as the only good signing ever made by former boss Graeme Souness, and is often referred to as the best player that Liverpool never had because he was rarely fit. Jones still managed to make over 200 appearances for the club, failing to score a goal in any.

Mercenaries

WHEN MIKE WALKER TOOK OVER AS MANAGER OF EVERTON in 1994 he was being tipped by many as a future England boss. His teams played a positive, attractive, attacking style of football that won him a lot of fans. But the truth is that his reputation was built over just two seasons as a first team manager with Norwich City. Granted, they did qualify for the UEFA Cup and beat German giants Bayern Munich while they were there, but this run of good form can probably be put down to a combination of pure dumb luck and a strong inherited squad that included Welsh international, Jeremy Goss, young striking sensation, Chris Sutton and exciting winger, Ruel Fox, rather than any particular moments of tactical genius from Walker. But this success meant that Everton were forced to pay Norwich a hefty compensation fee when they poached him in January 1994.

At the time, the Goodison club was struggling near the bottom of the Premier League and in need of a lift if they were to continue their 40 year run in the top tier of English football. But apart from a last day escape from relegation the Walker miracles never came, and after just 10 months in charge he was given the boot. So what had gone wrong? What did Mike Walker do differently from his time at Norwich, where he had so much success? What was missing from Mike Walker's Everton squad?

In the summer of 1994, after Everton's historic win over Wimbledon, Walker decided that a big name signing would be needed to help restore some faith in him around the club, a big name player that had already achieved great success in the hope that his confidence would rub off on the rest of the squad. The rumour quickly spread that a Brazilian World Cup winner would be joining and hopes among the fans were high that a Romario or Bebeto could be wearing the famous royal blue of Everton. In reality, there was no way that either of those players would make the move to the North West of England. And when Walker announced that he would be signing Brazilian international, Muller, you could almost hear the sound of a million Everton fans shout, "Who the bloody hell is that?" echo around Liverpool. But the guy was a member of the Brazil squad that had recently won the World Cup in America, and was also one of Sao Paulo's greatest ever goal scorers. There was no hiding it. Walker was delighted with his new acquisition and there was a definite buzz around the club leading up to the press conference. But half an hour before he was to be photographed wearing his new shirt, the 28 year old Brazilian had a change of heart and decided that Everton wasn't the club for him after all. It was a big embarrassment for Walker and the club, but when you look at the real reasons behind it you can't help but feel that Everton got away with making a big mistake, because he obviously wasn't signing for the right reasons in the first places.

It was thirty minutes before the big unveiling and the press had gathered to see the player being tipped as a saviour, but behind the scenes all was not going to well. It appears that Muller, or his advisers, had had another look at the contract and realized that he would still have to pay tax on his 20,000 GBP a week pay packet. And when the Everton board informed him that he would also have to buy his own house he stormed out, leaving Walker and Everton looking like a bunch of prized tossers, signing for Kashiwa Reysol in Japan's J League instead. It was pretty sad to see a player at just 28 and supposedly coming into his peak years opting for the easy money, but that is the way of the world at times, and his eight league goals in a less than impressive Japanese spell ruined any chance he would have had of proving himself on the big European stage.

What If?

EVERTON SIGNED BRAZILIAN WORLD CUP WINNER, MULLER, on the 1st of August 1994 with boss Mike Walker hoping that his winning mentality would become engrained on the rest of the squad. Going in to the opening game of the 1994-95 season against Aston Villa the atmosphere around Goodison Park was electric. The Everton fans were full of hope and optimism because they now had a future England boss in charge, and a Brazilian superstar leading the line. That optimism only increased when Muller's Everton career got off to a flying start as he lashed home a shot from the edge of the area to give his team the lead after just 5 minutes. From here Everton took total control, with Muller looking every bit the flashy South American as he caused problems for the Villa defence all afternoon. His first touch was outstanding as he showed an array of clever flicks and passes all topped off by a stunning hat-trick in the 4-1 Everton win. It was the complete debut and the victory had the critics raving about the new all out attacking style of the Tofees. Over the next month Everton looked the business, and by the end of September they were top of the league by two points with Muller having scored a fantastic 7 goals.

Although Everton were travelling well the football press were beginning to look at the lack of depth in the squad.

How would they replace the magnificent Muller if he were injured or suspended? Many names were lashed around as possible targets, but the one that just wouldn't go away was that of troubled Glasgow Rangers star, Duncan Ferguson.

Ever since his 4 million GBP British transfer record move from Dundee Utd the big Scot had found nothing but trouble. The fans never really took to him as he scored just two league goals and was soon replaced in the starting line-up by Gordon Durie. But the curtain finally fell on his Rangers career after he was prosecuted for a vicious head butt on Raith Rovers' John McStay, a crime that would later see him do time in Barlinnie prison. At the end of it Rangers wanted to be rid of him, and when they heard that Everton could be interested they were more than happy to let him go. While there was no way that Everton would pay the 4 million GBP asking price, Rangers offered the striker up on a three month loan deal. Everton accepted, and it looked like the move would soon go through with all the talk from the press being about the positive pressure that the signing would put on Muller. But it seemed that the Brazilian wasn't too fond of having his spot in the side put under any sort of threat, and he called an emergency meeting with his boss, Mike Walker. Walker tried his best to let Muller know that he was the first choice striker and that Ferguson was just cover. But Muller insisted that if Ferguson were to join, even on a loan deal, he would be walking out of the door. Walker crumbled. There was no way that he could risk losing his new star player so he told Rangers that Ferguson would not be coming to Goodison. For Duncan Ferguson the collapse of the move to Everton meant that he would have to find another way out of his Rangers nightmare. But it even came as a surprise to him when his saviour came from just 400m down the road from his original destination. Liverpool boss, Roy Evans, was looking to add some muscle and grunt to his own forward line and for him Everton's loss was Liverpool's gain and on the 31st of October 1994 Duncan Ferguson signed for Liverpool in a deal reportedly worth 3.75 million GBP.

While Liverpool were delighted with their new signing, for Everton the Muller dummy split was to be the first of many. After being substituted during a match against Wimbledon on the 2nd of January 1995 Muller stripped off his shirt and threw it to the Wimbledon fans, (who proceeded to tear it to pieces,) before walking straight into the stadium and out of the back door. No one knew where the Brazilian had got to, and it was a week before he returned to training without giving any explanation. The Everton fans were quick to forgive him, but the players were beginning to feel that he didn't really have the best interests of the club at heart.

On the pitch the team was beginning to struggle, and Walker felt that Muller had to play if they were to keep up their challenge for a European spot. The only problem was that with every good performance, and every goal, Muller would knock on his boss's door demanding higher pay and more bonuses. At first the Everton board caved in to his every whim, but as the goals dried up and the rest of the squad became disheartened by Muller's constant complaining, they decided enough was enough. After Muller scored a goal against Leicester City on the 4th of March 1995 he made the now regular trip to the manager's office after the game. The meeting was brief but precise; Muller simply said that if his wages were not increased by 10,000 GBP per week he would be leaving.

"I couldn't believe my ears," said Walker in a 2000 interview with *Four Four Two* magazine. "I tried to tell him that we would discuss it at the end of the season, but he wouldn't listen. He just tipped over my desk and stormed out." Muller was gone.

He turned up six months later, playing for former club Sao Paulo while officially still contracted to Everton. The Everton board tried their best to make him come back but it was too late. Everton finished the 1994-95 season in 10th position after losing the last six games of the season. The disappointment of such a poor run along with the off field problems saw team morale slip and after they failed to win any of the opening ten games at the start to the 1995-96 season manager Mike Walker was sacked. Asked during his interview with *Four Four Two* if signing a money grabbing mercenary such as Muller was his biggest mistake as Everton boss, Walker replied, "No, but I should have signed Duncan Ferguson."

"Sometimes I Dive, Sometimes I Stand"

ARSENE WENGER IS SEEN AS SOMETHING OF A MIRACLE worker when it comes to delving into the transfer market. He never seems to splash out big money on big name players; instead he looks for the rough diamonds that that no one else seems to want. He then polishes them until they are as close to perfect as possible and sells them on for a hefty profit, but not until they have helped him win a few trophies along the way. Since taking over as Arsenal manager in 1996 Wenger has signed players such as Nicolas Anelka for 500,000 GBP in 1997 before selling him on to Real Madrid in 1999 for a staggering 22.3 million GBP. He has also unearthed talents such as Cesc Fabregas, Emmanuel Adebayour, Ashley Cole and Patrick Vieira. And it was Wenger's astute football brain that saw Thierry Henry convert from a right winger to a centre forward with amazing success. But despite what people might think about Arsene Wenger, the miracle worker, there have been times when even he has fucked it up; only sometimes, though.

Didier Drogba was born on the 11th of March 1978 in, Abidjan, the largest city in the small African country of Cote d'Ivoire also known as the Ivory Coast. As a youngster, Drogba moved to France to live with his uncle before settling in Antony, a suburb of Paris after his family followed him over from The Ivory Coast when he was 15. Drogba had always enjoyed playing football but it was only now that that enjoyment turned into an obsession and he began dreaming of playing for French side Marseille. Drogba's large frame and instinctive goal scoring abilities soon landed him a contract with Ligue 2 team Le Mans, where he made his debut at 18, just three years after playing his first real match with a local school boy team. But Drogba was far from impressive in his early career and it wasn't until four years after his debut while playing for Guingamp that he began to really turn on the style. 20 goals in 45 league games secured his dream move to Marseille for 3.5 million GBP in 2003. In just one season he cemented himself as a legend at the club, scoring 19 goals and winning the French Leagues player of the year award. He was so loved by the fans at Marseille that they still sing his name at home games.

But his stay at the Stade Velodrome was short as English side, Chelsea, with their new boss the special one himself, Jose Mourinho, were desperate to bring Drogba to the Premier League. For Chelsea, money was no object and they told Marseille to name their price, so Marseille did, and in July 2004 Drogba moved to Stamford Bridge for a club record 24 million GBP. The move has proved to be money well spent as Drogba has helped the London club clinch a series Premier League titles, two FA Cups and a Champions League final appearance. But his success at Chelsea has been marred somewhat by claims that he cheats, going to ground to easily for someone with such a muscular frame in order to win his side penalties and free-kicks. Drogba even got himself into trouble by saying, "Sometimes I <u>dive</u>, sometimes I stand," in a post match interview. But no matter what people think of Drogba's antics, no one can deny that when at his best he is a devastating talent, and that most Premier League managers would sell their grandmothers to have him in their starting line-up.

Many people see Drogba as a late bloomer, a fine wine that has just got better with age. But there is one person who was impressed with Drogba even as he struggled to make an impact at Le Mans when he was just 18.

"We watched Drogba very carefully when he was at Le Mans and his value was just £100,000," said Arsene Wenger before his Arsenal side faced Chelsea in the 2009 FA Cup Semi Final. "But we felt at the time he might not be completely ready. Sometimes when you watch a striker playing in a scrappy Championship game you can think, 'Yes, he has something but...' And don't forget, we had Thierry Henry at that time. We continued to follow his progress but suddenly he moved to Guingamp, then to the club of his dreams at Marseille and then on to Chelsea. Looking back now, of course it was a mistake. But it is not just us who now have regrets. There were a lot of other clubs watching him then."

Oh well, Arsene! Here is a quick peek at just what the Henry-Drogba partnership could have brought you.

What If?

ON THE 15TH AUGUST 2001 ARSENAL SECURED THE SIGNING of promising Ivory Coast striker Didier Drogba for 100,000 GBP from small French Club Le Mans. Arsenal boss Arsene Wenger was so excited by the signing of his latest young superstar that he proclaimed, "The Henry-Drogba partnership is going to devastate the Premier League." Despite this bold claim Wenger didn't play the pair in the same team all season. In fact, Drogba made just three appearances in the 2001 – 2002 season, all as a substitute replacing Henry. It wasn't until the 1st January 2003 that

Wenger would unleash the pair in the same starting lineup, and the Arsenal fans would get to see the amazing abilities of the player that many had already forgotten about.

It was a top of the table clash against Chelsea. The tension around Highbury was immense as both teams needed all three points if they were to continue their league title campaigns. Chelsea came out fast, looking to put the home team on the rack. Joe Cole was at his sublime best, teasing and tormenting the Arsenal defence. In the tenth minute he picked the ball up on the left, played a one- two with Lampard and cracked a right foot shot against the foot of the post. Arsenal managed to scramble the ball away to the feet of Thierry Henry who went on a mazy run down the right, side stepping Claude Makelele before spraying a cross field ball to the chest of Didier Drogba. Drogba brought it down, then twisted and turned, trying his best to evade the attentions of Chelsea defender, John Terry. He shifted the ball on to his right foot and looked set to smash it past Carlo Cudicini in the Chelsea goal before going to ground from an innocuous looking challenge. He lay on the floor looking up starry eyed at the referee hoping for a penalty. Terry shook his head and motioned to the ref that Drogba had dived. The Chelsea fans were screaming for him to be punished and the ref duly obliged, showing him the yellow card. There were no complaints from Drogba who got to his feet and got on with the game, but the look on Arsene Wenger's face said it all. He wasn't happy at all with his young striker. Booing began from both Chelsea and Arsenal fans every time Drogba was near the ball as it looked like he was well and truly out of his depth.

Five minutes into the second half, and it was Chelsea who were once again on the attack. Lampard and Makelele were dictating the pace, winning tackles and dominating the entire proceedings. But after Makelele misplaced a pass, Arsenal sprung to the counter attack. Henry was bounding down the left when he spotted Drogba peeling off his marker on the back post. Henry floated an inviting cross over toward him and Drogba attacked it without fear. The header thundered off the underside of the bar and into the back of the net. The Arsenal players mobbed the goal scorer who seemed to grow in confidence as his presence up front began causing Chelsea all sorts of problems. He was powerful, held the ball up superbly well and was a great focal point for Thierry Henry to play off. Henry went on to score two as Arsenal cruised to a 3-0 victory. From here the new Arsenal strike partnership was truly devastating, scoring an amazing 32 goals between them and helping Arsenal finish the season top of the pile, 7 points ahead of Manchester Utd.

The 2003-2004 season started off pretty much the same way. Arsenal went unbeaten for the first eight games with Drogba scoring 10 goals and Henry 12. Suddenly there were rumours that Drogba was wanted by Real Madrid, Barcelona and Inter Milan. But on 10th January 2004, Arsenal boss Arsene Wenger decided to cash in on his new superstar by selling him to Chelsea who had been chasing the striker ever since he tore them apart just a year earlier. The fee was a phenomenal 25.6 million GBP, making Arsenal a total profit of 25.5 million in just two and a half years. Drogba went on to become a firm fans favourite at Stamford Bridge, but the football world couldn't help but marvel at the business brain of the masterful Arsene Wenger. The genius had done it again.

Football Genius?

People say footballers have terrible taste in music but I would dispute that. In the car at the moment I've got The Corrs, Cher, Phil Collins, Shania Twain and Rod Stewart.
                    ANDY GRAY ON SKY SPORTS

ANDY GRAY IS MOST FAMOUS FOR BABBLING BULLSHIT as a football pundit on English satellite channel, Sky Sports. But despite his sometimes nonsensical comments on the beautiful game, Gray has become a very popular figure among fans in the same way as Ron Atkinson or the late, great, Bobby Robson are, for always saying the wrong thing. However, many people think that his seeming lack of knowledge is all part of the show, spoken only to invoke a reaction from other pundits and the people he interviews, and that he is in fact a true football genius.

Andy Gray's football life began in Scotland playing for Dundee Utd in 1973. From the start, the big strong striker from Glasgow proved to be a massive handful for defenders. He was good in the air, quick on the floor and played the game with a fearless attitude that served him well throughout his career. After an unbelievable two years with Dundee in which he scored 46 goals in only 62 league appearances, a move south of the border was inevitable, and it was midlands club Aston Villa that snapped up the burley Scotsman in October 1975. He re-paid their faith in him by almost instantly winning the golden boot award in his first season, scoring 25 goals. For the 1976-77 season the 21 year old stepped it up a notch, and as a reward for his 29 league goals he was given both the PFA Young Player of The Year Award and PFA Player's Player of The Year Award. It was an unprecedented achievement that was unmatched until a certain Portuguese player by the name of Ronaldo was awarded the same double at the end of the 2006-07 season.

From there, Andy Gray's football career began to unravel a little as he failed to reach the heights of his first two seasons with Aston Villa. In 1979 Gray was sold to Wolverhampton Wanderers for a British record fee of 1.5 million GBP. But his time at Molineux was less than spectacular as the club was relegated from the first division in 1982. Gray did score the winning goal in the 1980 league cup final but a disappointing 38 league goals in his four years at the club saw him sold on to Everton for just 250,000 GBP. At Everton, Gray became something of a legend as he was a member of a successful squad that won the FA Cup league title and Cup Winners Cup. But in 1985 Everton signed a certain Gary Lineker, and Gray was sold back to Aston Villa for just 150,000 GBP. This move really signalled the end of Gray as a significant figure in the world of football. He bounced around from club to club, playing for Villa, Notts County, West Bromwich Albion, Glasgow Rangers and Cheltenham Town all in the space of three years. He failed to set any of them alight and in 1990 he seemed to disappear from the football scene for good.

Gray did make a cameo appearance as a coach at Aston Villa but he failed to achieve anything significant, and left the club after just one year. Then in 1992 Andy Gray popped up as a co commentator on the newly formed Sky Sports TV channel, sharing his tactical views on football with the world and making phrases such as, "Take a bow, son," and, "You don't save those," his very own. He quickly gained a cult following, but his new found popularity was not due to his insightful understanding of football. It was more because his ridiculous take on games, and obvious bias toward certain teams made him almost comical.

So, in 1997, when he was given the opportunity to manage former club Everton after Joe Royale's departure, it wasn't just the Everton fans that were hoping he would take up the post. The entire football community were intrigued to see if the man who seemed to have all the answers on TV, the man who would berate mangers and players alike for the decisions they made on the football field, really had what it took to manage at the top level.

Andy Gray himself was keen to test the managerial waters especially at a club where he had had so much success and was still hailed as a hero.

"In my heart I wanted to manage Everton. In many ways it would have been the realization of a dream," said Gray in an interview with *The Liverpool Echo* newspaper.

But just as it looked like he would put pen to paper on a deal, Gray was offered a contract reportedly worth around 20,000 GBP a week to remain at Sky Sports, and suddenly the pressures of football management didn't seem so appealing.

"Maybe I got a little carried away with all the speculation, and to take the job and then let the supporters down would have been too much to bear. Sky also held a unique place in my heart, and at the end of the day, to decide to continue my broadcasting career with them made it impossible for me to leave. It goes without saying that I wish Everton and their fans all the best for them this season and everyone at the club will always have a special place in my heart."

But his little speech didn't hold with Everton fans or Chairman Peter Johnson. "I am aghast that the man has behaved like this," said Johnson after hearing about Gray's decision. "It is quite difficult to believe and to take in. Andy Gray applied for the job, came to an interview with us and then went straight out from the interview and started talking about the job. We have been nothing other than the totally wronged party in this episode. What has happened has shocked me."

While his decision disappointed many in the game, Andy Gray is still managing to entertain the World with some fantastic comic moments. He is an entertainer and good at what he does.

"For my money, Duff servicing people from the left with his balls in there is the best option." Beautifully done, Andy, truly beautiful.

What If?

FOOTBALL PUNDIT ANDY GRAY WAS FINALLY UNVEILED as the Everton manager on 8th July 1997 after turning down a lucrative contract to stay on at Sky Sports.

"Everton has always been in my heart and it is an absolute honor to be leading this great club," said Gray, moments after putting pen to paper on a 5 year deal. He went on to say, "It is going to be hard work but my goal is get Everton back where they belong, or, at the very least, back above Liverpool."

The Everton fans lapped it up, and despite not making any new signings, and a less than impressive pre season, campaign hopes were high when they kicked off the 1997 –

98 season against Crystal Palace. But from the first minute it was obvious that Everton's problems had not been ironed out as Palace came racing out of the blocks, taking the lead inside five minutes. Everton never looked up to it and lost 3-0, much to the disappointment of their new manager who left the dug out on the 75th minute mark and disappeared back into the stadium. Asked in a later press conference where he had got to, Gray simply said, "I had business to attend to." Everton fans were in an uproar that he had left his post and not given a satisfactory explanation for his actions. Their anger only increased as Everton failed to win any of their first three games.

On 31st August Gray unveiled two new signings that he hoped would turn his disastrous start to the year around. The first was 18 year old Arsenal defender, Matthew Upson, on a year long loan deal, while the second was the surprise signing of Ghanaian international Nii Lamptey from Union de Santa Fe in Argentina. Some years earlier, Lamptey had been labeled as the new Pele after a string of stunning performances that led to Ghana winning the U17 World Cup. But despite impressing at spells with Belgian side Anderlecht and Dutch side PSV Eindhoven, Lamptey's career took a bit of a nose dive as he struggled to adjust to life in England after arriving in 1994. He made just ten appearances for Aston Villa and six for Coventry City before being sold to Venezia in Italy in 1996. But Andy Gray remembered him well from his Villa days, and had never forgotten that Lamptey had bucket loads of raw talent. "He's got it. There is no doubt about that. The boy has it all," he said as he unveiled his new signing. But the Everton fans weren't convinced and local radio shows were inundated by angry fans asking the question, "What is Andy Gray up to?"

By Christmas, Everton were struggling just four points off the relegation zone. And while Upson was performing well for his new club, Gray's only other signing was struggling to keep up with the pace of the English game, with his performances showing a total lack of confidence. After a shocking 5-0 defeat against Manchester Utd on Boxing Day in which Lamptey came on as a second half substitute only to be take off just ten minutes later, it was obvious that a crisis was slowly unfolding at Goodison Park, and that something needed to be done fast. Fans called for Gray to quit, while Gray called for more time. The Everton board went straight down the middle and gave him until the end of January to turn the club around. After another crushing 2-0 defeat this time against fellow strugglers Crystal Palace on 10th January 1998, the Everton fans decided enough was enough and thousands of them camped outside Goodison Park stating that they wouldn't leave until Gray was sacked. Marc Price who was a spokesman for the group said, "We appreciate that Andy has done his best. But if he loves the club as much as we do, he will realize that his best is just not good enough."

And when Andy Gray called a press conference for 9am on Monday the twelfth of January, most people thought that it would be to announce his resignation. But as he came out to face the country's press he was followed by none other than former Manchester Utd star Eric Cantona. Cantona had retired from football at the end of the 1996 – 97 season at just 30 years of age, stating that he wished to go out on top. But after much persuasion, over six months of secret meetings and hours of phone calls, Everton boss, Andy Gray had managed to attract Cantona to Goodison Park.

"I am pleased to announce that Eric Cantona will be joining the club as a player coach as of today," said Gray with a very smug grin across his face. The press went mental and as cameras flashed and questions rained out, Cantona made one simple statement, "I do not have to justify my decisions to you. I am here because I want to be here."

It was later revealed that Andy Gray had thought that the only thing lacking in his squad was confidence-confidence in him, each other and themselves, and he thought bringing in such a personality as Cantona would restore everyone's faith, including the fans.

"It's a step in the right direction," said fans spokesman Marc Price.

Despite him not even making the subs bench, the arrival of Cantona had an immediate positive effect on the team as they went unbeaten for the whole of February. The run included an amazing 3-0 win away to local rivals Liverpool, in which Nii Lamptey notched his first ever Everton goal. Cantona finally made his debut on the 14th of March 1998 against Blackburn and showed that he still had what it takes. It was like watching a master class as Cantona controlled the pace of the game with a grace that only a few players in history have possessed. But what was even more impressive, was the way the players around him responded especially, Nii Lamptey, who capped his man of the match display with two goals, as Everton romped home 4-1.

Everton ended the season in mid table, which was an astonishing achievement after the dramas at the start of the campaign. From here, Andy Gray and Eric Cantona began to slowly build an empire that the fans and all involved at the club believed they deserved. Nii Lamptey became one of the most feared players in Europe, attracting attention from the likes of Real Madrid and Barcelona. But in 1999 he pledged his future to the club, saying that without Everton he would probably be a "washed up nobody," and promptly signed a 10 year deal that would also see him move on to the coaching staff when his playing days were up. In 2000, Lamptey repaid the faith shown in him by the Everton fans and staff when he was awarded the European golden boot for his phenomenal 29 League goals. In 2002, Andy Gray resigned from the post, leaving Cantona to take over a squad that looked destined to challenge Manchester Utd as the dominant force in English football.

Busted Brazilian

RONALDINHO WAS BORN RONALDO DE ASSIS MOREIRA, on the 21st March 1980 in Porto Alegre Brazil. His upbringing was poor, and, as with most poor Brazilian families the Morerias saw football as their way out of poverty. Ronaldinho's father, Joao da Silva Moreira, played for amateur club Esporte Clube Cruzeiro, but it was his two sons that would make the step up to take on the professional ranks. Ronaldinho's older brother, Roberto, was considered a hot prospect at Brazilian club Gremio, and was even given a house with a swimming pool as down payment on what was surely going to be an amazing professional career. But tragedy was soon to strike the Moreira family. Ronaldinho's father drowned in the swimming pool at Roberto's house, and Roberto blew out his knee, prematurely ending his career and leaving his little brother Ronaldo to carry the burden of his entire family.

Ronaldo de Assis Moreira took on this weight of responsibility superbly and was soon picked up by the same club as his brother, Gremio, and broke into the first team in 1997 at the age of 17. He was now going by the nickname Ronaldinho, which means "The Little Ronaldo," and was causing a stir all around the footballing world. 21 goals in 44 games for Gremio saw Ronaldinho pull on the famous yellow shirt for Brazil, and in the 1999 Copa America he scored six times, with a goal against Venezuela, going down in history as one of the greatest ever Brazilian goals. His form soon attracted interest from all over Europe and in 2000 a move to French giants Paris Saint-Germain was arranged for around 5 million GBP. "The Little Ronaldo" literally had the world at his feet.

So you really have to wonder, just why, on the crest of this massive wave, the hottest property in world football nearly signed on loan for Scottish side St. Mirren.

St. Mirren were struggling to keep afloat in the Scottish Premier League at the time and were hoping to add some fire power to the side in an a attempt to stay in the big time. Their first options had been Nigerian Daniel Amokachi, Paul Kitson and controversial Italian, Benito Carbone, but they all turned down the move. St Mirren manager Tom Hendrie then said no to bringing Brazil legend Bebeto to Love Street because of doubts over his fitness. So, with Gremio's season already over, and Ronaldinho in a 6 month limbo until he officially moved to Paris, St. Mirren put together a sensational move for the buck-toothed footballing dynamo. Amazingly, their main selling point was to give Ronaldinho experience playing in a tough European league before his big move. But even more amazing was the fact that Ronaldinho fell for it and agreed to move to Love Street for a three month stint. The excitement around the club was unbelievable, but unfortunately for all involved at St. Mirren, the deal fell through after Ronaldinho was investigated for apparently holding a false passport. Having failed in their attempts to sign a big name forward to halt their slide in to the lower leagues, St. Mirren got Stephen McPhee from Coventry City instead. McPhee failed to score in his seven appearances, and St. Mirren finished at the bottom of the table with just 35 points.

From here, Ronaldinho went on to conquer the football world and cement his place as an absolute legend in the world game. In 2002 he helped Brazil win their fifth World Cup. In 2006 he won the European Champions League with Barcelona, on top of picking up the FIFA World Player of the year award twice, in 2004 and in 2005. He was also named European player of the year in 2005 and was selected in the UEFA team of the year on numerous occasions.

What If?

AFTER TWO MONTHS OF DISCUSSIONS, RONALDINHO finally made his St. Mirren debut at home against one of the giants of Scottish football, Glasgow Rangers, on 2nd January 2001. It was an icy cold afternoon at Love Street, and the rain was falling heavily with water logging the pitch. The young Brazilian was struggling to come to terms with the conditions and under the close attention of Rangers midfielder Barry Ferguson. But in the 40th minute he managed to escape his marker, and, after a clever flick and some quick feet, Ronaldinho found himself in some welcomed space. He looked up, ready to pick out a pass, only to have an overzealous Ferguson, out to save face, lunge in two footed from the side. A loud snap echoed around the stadium and a blood curdling scream rang out, leaving everyone in a stunned silence. Ronaldinho was laid out, motionless, face down in the mud. It actually took a few minutes for the severity of the situation to hit home and when it did, the crowd began to gasp with pure horror. Ronaldinho's legs were sticking out at funny angles and pieces of bone were sticking through his now blood red socks. Ferguson was frantically waving for the medical staff to come on to the pitch. When they arrived they went to work straight away, pulling the bones back in line and stemming the flow of blood that now seemed to be squirting all over the pitch. Ronaldinho was rushed to hospital where x-rays showed that he had broken both the tibia and fibula in three places in his right leg, while his left knee was dislocated and his medial ligaments destroyed.

The injury saw his dream move to Paris Saint-Germain collapse, and many people thought that the young superstar would never pull on his boots ever again. But after two years of rehabilitation, and a lot of guts, Ronaldinho made an amazing comeback for Gremio, the club where he started his career. While he was never quite the same player as before his horrific injury, he did put in some strong performances that secured him a move to Newcastle Utd in the English Premier League. Newcastle had hoped that he would rediscover some of his early magical form, but it never quite happened, and Ronaldinho became quite content to eat up his massive pay cheque with the rest of the underachieving squad and dream about the player he could, or should have been. He never played for Brazil again.

The 2002 World Cup

WHILE THIS WAS CERTAINLY A GREAT LOSS FOR THE WORLD of football, for England it actually had some positive knock on effects. On 21st June 2002, England faced off against Brazil at the quarter final stage of the World Cup in Japan and Korea. The teams had finished level at half time after goals from England's Michael Owen, and a superb finish in first half injury time effort from Rivaldo. It looked like it was going to take something special to separate the sides when, five minutes into the second half, Brazil were awarded a free kick in a dangerous position. But without Ronaldinho to fluke one over the head of England goal keeper David Seaman, it was up to Rivaldo to take the kick.

He stepped up and hit one high and not so handsomely over the bar. From the resultant goal kick England striker Michael Owen found himself with a half chance on the edge of the area only to be brought down by Brazil Captain Cafu. The free kick was in perfect David Beckham country, and the whole of England expected their talisman to produce something special. They all waited with baited breath as Beckham stepped up confidently, but his standing foot slipped and the kick went straight toward the Brazilian wall. It flicked off the heel of Ronaldo, wrong footed goal keeper Marcos, and trickled in to the bottom corner. England held on to win 2-1 and eventually won the title, humiliating the Germans 6-0 in the final.

You Can Do That to ME

FOR 12 YEARS, IRISH LEGEND, ROY KEANE, CONTROLLED the Manchester Utd midfield with both class and menace. He was respected by his team mates and feared by opponents throughout his 444 games, and is definitely one of the game's greatest ever players.

After apparently being knocked back a number of clubs including the likes of Liverpool and Aston Villa, Keane finally began his professional career at Nottingham Forest under the tutelage of the late great Brian Clough. Clough was renowned for his no nonsense style of management, and in Keane's autobiography he tells how a misplaced back pass during a 1991 FA Cup match against Crystal Palace resulted in Clough punching the young Irishman in the face.

"When I walked into the dressing room after the game, Clough punched me straight in the face... I was too shocked to do anything but nod in agreement," said Keane.

But despite taking a punch off his former manager, Keane has nothing but respect for the man that gave him one the most important football lessons of his career, "Brian Clough's advice to me before most games was: 'You get it, you pass it to another player in a red shirt'. That's really all I've tried to do at Forest and United— pass and move— and I've made a career out of it."

In 1993 at the age of 22, and after playing 123 times for

Forest, Keane, had become one of the most sought after players in the English Premier League. Forest had just been relegated, and were resigned to losing their midfield star, but they were never going to accept anything other than top dollar. A price of around 4 million GBP was placed on his head, which instantly ruled out a number of clubs including Liverpool and Arsenal who were simply unable to afford what would have been a British record transfer fee. But there was one club that could easily scrape up that sort of cash and more if need be, Blackburn Rovers. Keane quickly agreed terms to join Kenny Dalglish and his up and coming club, but before he signed anything he decided to take a little holiday back in Ireland to see his family. While he was there he received a phone call that would quite simply change his life. Manchester Utd boss, Alex Ferguson, called Keane at his family home and told him not to sign anything with Blackburn until they had spoken. Alex Ferguson's powers of persuasion were simply phenomenal; he told the Irishman that although United would win the league with or without him, if he did join him at Old Trafford they would also win the Champions League. For Keane who had been a United fan as a boy, and who had just watched them clinch their very first Premier League title in style, this show of faith was all he needed to hear, and there was now only one club that he wanted to sign for.

United decided to use Keane's eagerness to join them to their advantage, and tabled a 3.75 million GBP bid, which was 250,000 GBP lower than that bid by Blackburn. But with Keane now determined to sign for Manchester United, Nottingham Forest had no choice but to accept. The news of Roy Keane's U-turn did not impress Blackburn manager, Kenny Dalglish, who let fly with a vein popping tirade that apparently included, "Do you know who I am?" and, "You can't do that to Kenny Dalglish," as well as a number of swear words that I dare not repeat. But it was too late, and a new era had begun at Manchester United.

Keane made his debut on the 18th of August 1993, scoring twice in a 3-0 win against Sheffield Utd. By the end of the 1993 – 94 season, Keane had helped Utd. win their second league title in two years, establishing himself in midfield alongside Paul Ince. Over his 12 year Manchester career, Keane, would end up with 7 Premier League titles, 4 FA Cups and a Champions League winners medal. But despite all his obvious success, Keane's career has also been full of controversy.

Apart from his on field explosions that resulted in him being sent off 13 times during his career, there were also a number of very public off field incidents that made the headlines. In 2000, after a particularly subdued atmosphere during a Champions League victory against Dynamo Kiev, he criticised the very fans that had that been worshipping him since 1993 by saying, "Away from home our fans are fantastic. I'd call them hardcore fans, but, at home, they have a few drinks and probably the prawn sandwiches, and they don't realise what's going on out on the pitch. I don't think some of the people who come to Old Trafford can spell 'football', never mind understand it."

This was followed by his retirement from international football in 2002 when he stormed out of Ireland's World Cup squad just days before they were due to play their first game. Keane had told an Irish newspaper that their facilities were not up to scratch and that their preparations had been a joke. Ireland manager, Mick McCarthy, was not happy that one of his senior players had gone public with his grievances and demanded a face to face with Keane. But after Keane said, "Mick, you're a liar.... You're a fucking wanker. I didn't rate you as a player, I don't rate you as a manager, and I don't rate you as a person. You're a fucking wanker and you can stick your World Cup up your arse. The only reason I have any dealings with you is that somehow you are the manager of my country! You can stick it up your bollocks," before storming out, McCarthy wished he hadn't bothered.

It was this fiery temper and demand for perfection that served him so well throughout his career, and if someone had managed to stamp it out of him I am sure he would not have been the same player. But how would Kenny Dalglish and Blackburn Rovers have dealt with such a hostile talent?

What If?

ROY KEANE JOINED KENNY DALGLISH AND HIS Blackburn Rovers revolution on 1st August 1993 for a British record 4 million GBP. Dalglish was hoping that the feisty Irishman would provide the midfield steel that his side needed, behind a free scoring Alan Shearer. Keane made his debut against Chelsea on 14th August 1993 and wowed his new set of fans with dominant display, creating one goal and scoring another in a romping 3-0 win. But it was his ability to break up the opposition's attacks that had his new manager foaming at the mouth.

"His debut against Chelsea was easily the best performance I have ever seen from someone making their debut," said Dalglish in a 2001 interview with *The Daily Star* newspaper. "He won tackles, scored a goal and didn't misplace a pass all game. He was simply phenomenal."

With Keane dictating the midfield and Shearer on a record breaking goal scoring run, Blackburn won the first ten games of the 1993 – 94 season. And they were still top of the league by ten points at Christmas, but an incident in a Boxing Day match against Manchester Utd would change the course of their season and Keane's career.

After just two minutes it was obvious that Manchester midfielder Paul Ince had been given the task of roughing up

Keane, in an attempt to break up the Blackburn style of play. Keane picked up the ball on the half way line and attempted to break forward, but Ince never gave him the chance, sliding in two footed, taking both of the Irishman's legs from under him. Ince was given a yellow card for the incident, but Keane was carried from the field, his hands over his face, blood seeping through his socks and would apparently not be returning. But after playing for ten minutes with ten men, Keane was stood on the side of the pitch looking ready and raring to go. "I had a gash on my leg that needed 10 stitches," remembered Keane in his 2001 autobiography. "There was no way I was going to stay off the pitch. I told the physio to stitch me up and I went back into the action with only one thing in mind, revenge." Keane hobbled around the pitch for five minutes, and, with midfielder Paul Warhurst warming up on the side line, it looked as though Dalglish would pull him out of the action, but that decision would soon be taken out of his hands. Blackburn goal keeper, Tim Flowers, kicked the ball down the field, but it landed straight at the feet of Paul Ince. Ince didn't even have a chance to think what to do next as Roy Keane flew in knee high. Keane didn't even wait for the red card to be shown as he stood, took off his shirt and walked from the pitch. Keane was later banned from football for a month and fined 20,000 GBP for the horrific tackle. Blackburn manager Kenny Dalglish was disgusted by the incident and in a post match press conference he laid into his player calling him "an animal". But Keane didn't take to well to the public criticism and the following day questioned his boss' management labelling him "an overrated player that had fast become an overrated manager, that isn't fit to wipe Brian Clough's arse."

"I simply didn't mean what I said," said Keane in his autobiography. "At the time I was just very angry that he didn't back me up and criticized me in public." And it seems that Keane wasn't the only one that didn't like being talked about in the press. After reading what had been said about him over his morning cup of coffee and a bacon sandwich, Dalglish phoned his player simply to give him an earful. "Kenny called me up on a Wednesday morning, going totally mad," remembers Keane. "He was saying "You can't do that to Kenny Dalglish, you arrogant, Irish prick." I couldn't even get a word in and by the end of it he told me I was on the transfer list." Two months later Keane was sold for a cut price 2 million GBP to Spanish giants Real Madrid. Keane settled in straight away to his Spanish surroundings and was made captain of the club in 1995. All in all Keane won 10 league titles and 6 Champions League medals in his 12 years at the club, making him one of their most successful players of all time, before becoming their manager in 2006.

Keane's admission in his autobiography that what he had done was intentional, caused a wave of controversy around the world, but it also brought criminal charges against him after Paul Ince, who missed the next year and a half of football with an horrific broken leg and knee ligament damage, sued the Irishman for damages. In 2003 an out of court settlement was reached, thought to have been in the region of 1.5 million GBP. Questioned at the time about Paul Ince and the money, Keane simply said, "The Guvnor, my arse! He is just a big poof."

The Worst Premiership Players of All Time

IN RECENT YEARS THE ENGLISH PREMIER LEAGUE HAS become known as the greatest league in the world. Its fast flowing competitive style and amazing wealth is now attracting some of the best players in the history of the game. Players such as Portuguese superstar Ronaldo, Brazilian Robinho, Ukrainian Andriy Shevchenko, Germany's Jurgen Klinsmann and the Welsh wizard Ryan Giggs regularly grace English fields producing the best that the beautiful game has to offer. But the forays into the foreign transfer markets by Premiership clubs haven't always been too successful, and the league has also showcased players that would be lucky to warm the bench on a Sunday morning for my local booze house, The Punch Bowl. Here is a quick rundown of the worst that I have ever seen.

Bosko Balaban

FORMER ASTON VILLA CHAIRMAN, "DEADLY" DOUG ELLIS, very rarely entrusted his cheque book in the hands of his Managers, and when you look at the Bosko Balaban affair you can understand why. It was a muppet by the name of

John Gregory that talked Ellis into signing the lumbering Croatian for a whopping 6 million GBP in 2001. That extortionate fee was thanks mainly to few international goals and 38 in 55 league games for Croatian power house Dinamo Zagreb. While that seems like a pretty impressive record, if you take into account that the Croatian league is probably a step below the Scottish Premier League in terms of quality, you will begin to scratch your head as to where the huge figure came from. But Aston Villa paid it, and Balaban played out his 20,000 GBP a week, three year contract making only 9 appearances, seven of those as a substitute, without scoring a goal before signing for Belgian side Club Brugge on a free. The whole deal ended up costing the midlands club in excess of 1 million GBP a game, and while some may think it a bit mean to jump down John Gregory's throat over the deal you have remember that he also spent 9.5 million GBP of Doug Ellis's hard earned drug money on Columbian Juan Pablo Angel. And he wonders why he can't find a job in football anymore.

Djimi Troare

THE CLUMSY FRENCHMAN WAS LABELLED THE NEW Marcel Desailly when he was signed by Liverpool manager, Gerard Houllier in 1999. But instead of performing in the same calm and composed manner as the French World Cup winner, Traore looked more like a malnourished dog forced on to the field by a cruel owner in order to earn small portions of food. His obvious nerves, every time he was forced into action, saw him crumble under the pressure, and scoring own goals became common, as did giving away penalties by throwing around wild challenges. But despite making my list of the Premierships worst ever players, Traore somehow managed to grab himself a European

Champions League winners medal in 2005. Nice one, Djimi.

Istvan Kozma

M ANY L IVERPOOL FANS BLAME G RAEME S OUNESS for the clubs fall from the pinnacle of English football, and when you look at the players he brought to the club you can begin to see why. Souness was given the Liverpool job after a successful stint as manager of Glasgow Rangers. His success at Ibrox was mainly down to a big, fat cheque book that he used to bring England stars from south of the border. He also used the fact that English clubs had just been banned from European competition as another draw. But his ability to bring top players to Scotland, and his subsequent success only disguised the fact that he is no tactical genius, and that he wouldn't know real talent if it jumped up off the floor and smacked him in his big, bushy head.

He took over at a Liverpool club that was in slight decline and in definite need of some tweaking, but Souness went a bit spastic with his renovations, replacing Peter Beardsley with Dean Saunders, Ray Houghton with Paul Stewart, and was telling everyone that would listen that Lee Jones was the new Ian Rush and saw Mark Walters as the ideal replacement for John Barnes. On top of all of this he paid 300,000 GBP for Hungarian international, Istvan Kozma, from Scottish side Dunfermline. The press struggled to understand what it was that Souness was playing at, and after Kozma pulled on his Liverpool shirt for the first time, the Anfield faithful were also questioning Souness's ability. Kozma looked painfully out of his depth and thankfully managed only 6 appearances before being released in July 1993.

Ade Akinbiyi

AKINBIYI CAME TO PROMINENCE SCORING SPECTACULAR goals for Wolverhampton Wanderers in the 1999-2000 season, and finishing as their top marksman with 16 goals. Despite his impressive performances the Wolves missed out on promotion and were forced to sell their star striker for 5.5 million GBP to Leicester City. But as Andy Gray once famously said about Kevin Davies after his move from Southampton to Blackburn Rovers for 7.5 million GBP in 1998, "Scorers of great goals don't always make great goal scorers," and so it was for Akinbiyi. After 58 first team appearances for his new club he had managed just 11 goals. His woeful displays were soon picked up by the press who hounded everything he did, and before long the Filbert Street faithful had labelled him as Ade Akin-bad-buy-i. Ade's career has never recovered from his hell at Leicester City and after unsuccessful spells with Crystal Palace, Burnley and Sheffield Utd he moved to America and signed for Major League Soccer team, The Houston Dynamo, where he failed to score after 13 appearances. Give it up Ade, because you really are as bad as everyone is telling you.

Ali Dia

ALI DIA HAS TO BE THE CHEEKIEST LITTLE SHIT TO EVER PULL on a pair of football boots. After floating around the cut throat world of amateur football and failing trials at Port Vale, Gillingham and Bournemouth, in 1996, Dia, now 30 years old, was beginning to see his dreams of becoming a professional footballer slip away from him. So he and his agent came up with a plan that would give his career a little push in the right direction. Dia's agent phoned English Premier League club, Southampton, pretending to be former FIFA world player of the year, George Weah. He went on to say that Dia was his cousin, had 13 international caps for Senegal and was formally signed with Paris Saint-Germaine. But rather than check this big pile hoss out, Southampton fell for it hook, line, sinker and copy of angling times, giving Dia a one month contract to prove himself. He made his debut on 23rd November 1996 against Leeds Utd coming on as a substitute in the 32nd minute. But it didn't take long for the Southampton manager to realize his mistake and Dia was pulled off just 20 minutes later. Southampton superstar Matthew Le Tissier remembers the incident well. "He came to training on the Friday morning, played in a five aside match and nobody thought he was any good. So it was a big surprise the next day when he was named on the subs bench. After about 30 mins I suffered a calf strain and had to come off and Dia came on in my place. He looked like Bambi on ice as he ran around, which was actually very embarrassing to watch, as it probably was for the man who signed him." And who was the gullible twat of the day? It could only be the master of transfer fuck ups, the one and only Graeme Souness.

Ramon Vega

SWISS INTERNATIONAL RAMON VEGA SIGNED FOR LONDON club, Tottenham Hotspur, from Italian side Cagliari for 3.75 million GBP in 1997. He was signed by countryman Christian Gross (See worst managers in premiership history) and his arrival was supposed to sure up a leaky Spurs defence. But after some shaky performances it was pretty evident that Vega had attended the same football school as Liverpool's Djimi Traore. The English press quickly jumped on Vega's back giving him the nickname "Princess Vega" and ridiculed him for every little mistake. He did manage to see out four years at White Heart Lane before going out on loan to Celtic and signing for Watford in 2001. But his accident prone performances at Tottenham had permanently damaged the poor guy's confidence and after just one year at Vicarage Road he slipped into the depths of French football playing 23 games for Creteil before retiring in 2003.

Corrado Grabbi

IN 2001 MY OLD MATE GRAEME SOUNESS WAS AT IT again when he signed Corrado Grabbi from Ternana, a little known Italian side, for an amazing fee of 6.75 million GBP. Grabbi had already bounced around a number of Italian clubs, failing to set any of them alight. So you have to wonder what made Souness splash out such an outlandish transfer fee. Did he have shit in his eyes? Did he have a love of trying to bring the best out of seemingly average players? Or did he simply have no fucking idea about what it was he was doing? Whatever it was, Corrado Grabbi and his two goals in 30 games for Blackburn becomes the third Souness signing to make the top ten worst ever Premiership players list with more to come.

Massimo Taibi

ITALIAN GOAL KEEPER MASSIMO TAIBI WAS PUT ON THIS earth for one reason and one reason only, to prove that even Sir Alex Ferguson has bad days. Up until Taibi joined Manchester Utd for 4.4 million GBP from Venezia in 1999, Ferguson had made only minor mistakes when delving into the transfer market and even his bad signings were proving good enough to win league titles. But after the retirement of Peter Schmeical, who was probably the best ever Utd Keeper, Ferguson was struggling to find a suitable replacement. The cocaine fuelled Aussie, Mark Bosnich, was signed on a free from Aston Villa to fill the void, but his performances were unpredictable, brilliant one minute, a Graeme Souness signing the next. It didn't take long for Ferguson to search elsewhere, but little did he know that his next effort would become one of football's biggest jokes. Taibi was literally thrown in at the deep end with his debut match being against one of Utd's feistiest rivals, Liverpool. It didn't take long for the butter fingered Italian to show the Old Trafford faithful what would be in store when he ventured a long way from his goal in order to collect a wayward free kick. Taibi totally misjudged it and the ball slipped through his hands right onto the head of Liverpool's Sami Hyppia who nodded the ball into the empty net. Not many people know that Taibi actually went on to claim the man of the match award in that game with Utd winning 3-2, but it proved to be the height of his Manchester career. After conceding five goals against Chelsea and diving over a Matthew Le Tissier daisy cutter, which has become a YouTube favourite, he was christened "The Blind Venetian" and Ferguson decided to cut his losses, sending him back to Italy in disgrace.

Torben Piechnik

AFTER ALAN HANSEN RETIRED FROM FOOTBALL IN 1991, Liverpool have produced a number of centre backs that could have easily made this list. In 1989 they signed Swedish international Glen Hysen for 300,000 GBP from Fiorentina. Hysen came to Liverpool with a massive reputation as a no nonsense defender with a great ability to read the game. He had nearly signed for Manchester Utd in the same year, only for Liverpool to steal him from under their noses. Utd signed Gary Pallister instead, which proved to be the better move as Hysen struggled to cope with the pace of the English game. Nicky Tanner was bought from lower league side Bristol Rovers in 1988 in the hope that the 23 year old would learn from the more experienced heads around him and become a natural replacement for Hansen who was beginning to struggle with injury. But Tanner never reached the heights expected of him and was forced to retire in 1994 due to his own injury problems. But by far the worst Hansen replacement was Denmark's Torben Piechnik who was brought to Liverpool in 1992 by Graeme "I think I should stop smoking crack," Souness. From his first game it was plainly obvious to anyone with eyes that Piechnik was not equipped to cope with top flight English football. It took 2 years and 17 sloppy appearances for the player himself to realize that he had no future at Liverpool and he handed in a transfer request before heading back to Denmark.

Stephane Guiv'arch

Graeme Souness has taken a lot of stick in this section for his talent spotting abilities and for bringing about the downfall of Liverpool Football Club. But if the truth be known, Kenny Dalglish, the man Souness replaced at Liverpool, could just as easily have taken up most of this list. Before leaving Anfield, Dalglish made such shocking signings as Jimmy Carter and David Speedie. At Blackburn he signed Mike Newell and Paul Warhurst and then, during his disastrous spell at Newcastle, there was the lazy Swede, Andreas Anderson and Frenchman, Stephane Guiv'arch.

Guiv'arch has to be the worst player to ever win a World Cup, "But at least he has one," I hear you say. The truth is that he only holds the medal after being carried through the 1998 finals, in which he played as lone striker failing to score in all seven games, by an amazing squad that included the likes of Zinadine Zidane, Marcel Desailly and Emmanuel Petit. However, he did have an impressive domestic record that secured him a move to English Premier League side, Newcastle Utd. His time there is one that I am sure he would rather forget, as he played just four first team games managing just a single goal. Guiv'arch then signed for Glasgow Rangers in Scotland hoping that a drop in class may make it easier to score goals and help him back in to the French national squad, but after just five goals in 14 league games he was shipped back to France with his tail between his legs.

So there we have it— ten players that somehow managed to worm their way into top flight English football only to be put back in their place pretty sharpish, by what is without doubt the best domestic league in the world.

Red or Blue

S<small>TEVEN</small> G<small>ERRARD</small> <small>WAS BORN ON THE</small> 30TH <small>OF</small> M<small>AY</small> 1980 in Huyton Liverpool. From an early age he was simply surrounded by football with both Liverpool and Everton, who are separated by nothing more than 400 meters of park land in the heart of the city, dominating English football throughout the mid eighties. Despite Gerrard's claims that Liverpool was always his only team, there is a photo floating around of him as a boy wearing the blue of Everton that is always brought out by Evertonians when the two sides meet. It is thought that he changed his allegiance to the red side of the city after his ten year old cousin, Jon-Paul Gilhooley, who was a fanatical Liverpool fan, was killed in the 1989 Hillsborough disaster. To this day he dedicates his playing career to his lost cousin. "It was difficult knowing one of your cousins had lost his life," Gerrard said. "Seeing his family's reaction drove me on to become the player I am today." Gerrard ends his 2006 autobiography by saying, "I play for John-Paul."

But whether he was a red or blue as a boy doesn't really matter as it was Liverpool that brought him in to their youth academy as a nine year old after spotting him playing for local side Whiston Juniors. Although he showed some promise as a youngster he never looked like he was going to set the world alight. He failed to make any of the England youth squads and it even looked as if Liverpool were going let him go, and Gerrard attended several trials with other teams including one with Manchester Utd. Gerrard later claimed that this was to "pressure Liverpool" into giving him a YTS contract. His plan worked and Gerrard eventually made his professional debut on 29th November 1998 against Blackburn Rovers. Gerrard himself admitted that his early performances were nothing special and it wasn't until he put in an amazing display (albeit at right back) against Everton that he started to win over the Liverpool faithful.

Despite a few early injury problems that were put down to severe growing pains, the rise of Steven Gerrard was immense. He made his England debut against the Ukraine on the 31st of May 2000, played a key part in Liverpool winning the UEFA Cup, FA Cup and League Cup in 2001 and was made captain of the club in 2003. But after Liverpool had a disappointing 2003- 2004 season, failing to win a trophy, and finishing a long way off, the League leaders boss, Gerard Houllier, quit, leaving Gerrard to wonder in what direction the club would be heading.

At the same time a Russian billionaire by the name of Roman Abramovich had bought the Chelsea Football Club, and stated that money would be no object in his quest to lift the Premiership title. With the Abramovich cheque book well and truly open and with rumours rife that Gerrard wanted out of Liverpool, Chelsea tabled a 20 million GBP bid for his services. The saga of will he/won't he make the switch continued for a few weeks before Gerrard was persuaded to give the new Liverpool boss Rafael Benitez a chance, and to see where the club was at the end of the new season. His decision to stay proved vital for Liverpool as he scored a late goal against Olympiacos to keep their Champions leagues hopes alive before producing miracles in the final to helping the club win the Holy Grail of football for the fifth time in their history. But despite their success in Europe Liverpool struggled in the Premier League finishing 5th behind Everton and with his contract ending soon, the English press predicted that Gerrard would soon make the move to Stamford Bridge for around 30 million GBP. Asked about the situation straight after Liverpool's Champions League success Gerrard said, "How could I leave after a night like this?" But after Liverpool turned down another big money offer from Chelsea, Gerrard shocked the football world by handing in a transfer request turning down a contract reportedly worth 100,000 GBP a week. All at Liverpool had accepted the loss with Chief Executive Rick Parry stating, "Now we have to move on. We have done our best, but he has made it clear he wants to go and I think it looks pretty final". But the story hadn't finished there, as the very next day Gerrard put pen to paper on a new four year deal at Anfield. The official reason for the amazing change of heart was put down to a simple miscommunication by the club, but rumors around Liverpool were that something more sinister had taken place. The Gerrard family had had ties to the seedy underworld of Liverpool's organised crime in the past and it seemed that this world had suddenly turned on the England international. There were reports of death threats made against his family, and gangland orders to shoot Gerrard in the legs should he leave. But while it is well known that Gerrard has mixed with local Liverpool personalities that can be considered, 'a little bit dodgy,' in the past, I feel his decision to stay came from nothing more than a desire to help rebuild the club, to honor the memory of his cousin, and his transfer request only came after frustrations that contract negotiations slowed down. "I fully intended to sign a new contract after the Champions League final but the events of the last five or six weeks have changed all that," he said shortly after handing in his transfer request.

Gerrard has gone on to become one of the greatest

players in the world, was ranked second behind Kenny Dalglish in a poll of 100 players that shook the Kop and is being lined up by many as the next Liverpool manager. But there is no doubt that it all came very, very close to being so very different for the man from Huyton.

What If?

STEVEN GERRARD'S 35 MILLION GBP MOVE TO BIG spenders Chelski broke the hearts of Liverpool fans all over the world. It came on the back of his sublime performance in the 2005 European Champions League final in which he inspired his side to an amazing comeback against AC Milan as they clinched their fifth European title. Liverpool had found themselves 3-0 down at half time after Kaka and Hernan Crespo had simply torn them apart. But Gerrard pulled one back with a glancing header early in the second half and after 90 minutes the scores were level with Liverpool sealing the victory after a penalty shootout.

Everyone at Liverpool was hopeful that they could build on this success with Gerrard as the pivot around which a league title challenge could be built. But the draw of big money and almost guaranteed success proved too much for Gerrard and on 15th July 2005, his move to Stamford Bridge was completed.

While Liverpool fans were left crying in their pints of Stella, for the neutral the move brought together the mouth watering midfield combination of the goal scoring Chelsea legend Frank Lampard and the dynamic Gerrard. Although the pair had failed to perform together at international level the football press were left creaming in their brown and cream trim y-fronts because now the two England superstars would be guided by the self proclaimed special one, Jose Mourinho.

The pair were unleashed against Wigan on 14th August 2005, but despite the hype the Chelsea side struggled to click into gear while both Gerrard and Lampard were often caught out in advanced positions leaving acres of space behind for Wigan to exploit. Chelsea were lucky that the Wigan threat was only coming from the likes of Jason Roberts and Josip Skoko and not a young Wayne Rooney or Ronaldo, and they held on for a 0-0 draw. The poor Chelsea performance was written off as a case of opening day nerves and everyone expected Jose to iron out the problems for their next game against Arsenal. But things didn't improve and Arsenal easily steam rollered Chelsea 4-0. The Stamford Bridge crowd was not impressed with what they had seen and after Fabregas drilled home the fourth, the stadium quickly emptied.

Mourinho quickly jumped to the defence of his troops but for the next match he wielded the axe and it was his new signing, Steven Gerrard, that missed out. Gerrard was nothing but a bit part player for the next few weeks, and as his departure from the starting lineup coincided with an improvement in results for Chelsea, the English press quickly jumped on the former Liverpool player's back calling for him to be axed from the England squad. England Manager, Sven Goran Erikson, buckled under the pressure and Gerrard was omitted from his plans. Gerrard hit back by scoring two in a second half substitute appearance against Aston Villa and creating a third as Chelsea strolled to a 5-1 victory. But his virtuoso performance was labelled as 'too little, too late' by the press who had already lined Gerrard up for a cut price move back to Liverpool. Mourinho insisted that Gerrard was "not for sale at any price," and that he still had a massive part to play in his plans. But Mourinho left Gerrard out of the side for the game against his former club Liverpool on the second of October 2005.

From the first whistle Gerrard's name rang out from the Anfield crowd, and despite the reds going down to two early goals the chant didn't stop. After about thirty minutes Gerrard was asked to warm up by boss Jose Mourinho. He stepped out of the dugout, jogged down to the famous Kop end and began applauding the Liverpool fans for their support. This angered the Chelsea supporters who quickly began booing and gesturing toward the man that they had hoped would help them seal their third Premier League title in a row. Gerrard didn't emerge from the tunnel for the second half and the rumours were that he was off completing his sensational return to the club where he was still worshipped. Whether he was or not, there was no doubting that his time at Chelsea was well and truly up.

Reports were that Chelsea would be happy to sell Gerrard for 20 million GBP, almost half what they had paid for him only a few months earlier. But Liverpool had spent half of the money they received from the original transfer on signing Owen Hargreaves from Bayern Munich to fill the hole left by Gerrard, while the rest of the money went on clearing some outstanding debts with the bank. This left them in quite a pickle; desperate to get Gerrard back to the club, they tried everything from negotiating part exchange deals to promising a long term payment plan. But the truth was that Liverpool didn't have anyone that Chelsea wanted, and Chelsea wanted to recoup as much money as possible right away. So with the deal to take him back to Liverpool falling through, Steven Gerrard signed for AC Milan, the team he had helped defeat in the Champions League Final just eight months earlier, on 14th January 2006 for 20 million GBP.

From his very first game for The Rossanari, Gerrard looked back to his best. He seemed to thrive playing alongside Brazilian superstar Kaka, and a hat-trick against Empoli on 4th March 2006, as well as a brace in the last game of the season against Parma earned him a recall to the England squad for the 2006 World Cup in Germany.

England went in to the competition with high hopes. They were expected to qualify easily from their group that included Paraguay, Trinidad and Tobago and Sweden, and they got off to the perfect start albeit with a scratchy 1-0 win over Paraguay. Gerrard didn't feature in the game. In fact, England boss, Erikson didn't use the in-form midfielder at all as they cruised through the group, finishing top with seven points. Gerrard was even left out of the 1-0 second round win over Ecuador. But they had failed to set the tournament alight and it was obvious that something would have to change if they were to overcome power-horses Portugal in the quarter finals. The English press that had slammed Gerrard earlier in the season were now calling for him to be reinstated. But the debate still raged- could Gerrard and Lampard play together in the same team? Erikson clearly thought that they couldn't and once again it was Gerrard that was left on the bench.

There was nothing between the two sides after an hour's play, but the balance soon shifted in favour of the Portuguese when England forward, Wayne Rooney, was sent off for an inauspicious stamp on Portugal defender, Ricardo Carvalho. There were arguments as to the intent of Rooney's actions, but, intentional or not, England were down to ten men. Rather than the expected move to bring on another forward in the shape of Peter Crouch, England manager Erikson called on Steven Gerrard to fill the role. While this looked like England would be happy to sit it out and hope for penalties or a lucky breakaway goal, Erikson had other plans for the Milan superstar. Gerrard was told to push forward, close down and tackle hard. From the moment he stepped onto the field it was evident that his hunger and desire was far beyond that of anyone else on the pitch and Portugal struggled to cope with his pure energy.

His new role also pushed Lampard back into a more defensive role, which he took to better than anyone could have expected, controlling the pace of the game by keeping it simple and making Portugal chase the ball. Despite being a man down, England looked comfortable, but n spite of all their hard work they couldn't seem to get a breakthrough. It wasn't until later on, that their hard work paid off. It came after a long nothing ball forward by Frank Lampard fell right to the feet of Portugal defender, Ricardo Carvalho, who brought the ball down and looked up, ready to pick out a pass. But the few seconds that he stalled proved to be fatal and Gerrard had closed him down before he even knew he was there. Gerrard slid in, blocking the attempted clearance. As Carvalho fell over the top of him the ball broke loose on the edge of the Portugal box. Gerrard got to his feet and chased the ball down. Portuguese goal keeper Ricardo quickly became aware of the danger and advanced from his line to stop Gerrard from getting a clear shot on goal. But Gerrard got to the ball first and flicked it past the advancing keeper who clattered into Gerrard's legs, sending him tumbling in the box. Replays seemed to show that the initial contact was outside the penalty area, but referee Horacio Elizondo judged that it was inside and awarded England a penalty. It was Frank Lampard that was given the duty and he tucked it away into the bottom right corner giving Ricardo no chance and booking England's spot in the semi finals.

Gerrard's superb performance as a lone striker stirred up hope within all the football writers in England. And the man that they once lambasted as a waste of space during his time at Chelsea was now being seen as England's saviour and only hope for World Cup Success. Britain's *Independent* newspaper wrote: "Gerrard's performance against Portugal was like witnessing the second coming of Christ. There is no doubt in my mind that he has been sent down as a son of the football gods to save our souls, restore calm and help us claim the World Cup."

And it seemed that Sven Goran Erikson saw it the same way and Gerrard was named in the England Starting lineup for the first time in almost a year. His inclusion in the World Cup semi-final team to face France didn't come as a shock, but what did ruffle a few feathers was the fact that rather than play him up front to inject the same sort of intensity that he produced against Portugal, it seemed he would once again be given the holding midfield role behind Lampard, while Peter Crouch would play as a lone striker. The move failed, as Gerrard looked stifled in his new restricted role and was eventually taken off as the French took control and scored twice through Zinadine Zidane and Thierry Henry. Gerard was taken off with 20 minutes to go and while the English did score a late consolation goal from a Rio Ferdinand header, their World Cup dream was over for another year.

Gerrard continued to prosper at Milan before being transferred to Real Madrid along with team mate Kaka in 2009 for a whopping combined fee of 120 million GBP. But despite his success at club level the continued attempts by England manager's to play him along side Lampard as the defensive midfielder, and the constant criticism this brought from the English press for every poor England performance frustrated him, and he retired from the international side in May 2007, four days before his 27th birthday.

The Scouse Perm

As I said before, throughout this book, I have given Graeme Souness a hell of a lot of stick, especially when it comes to his totally inept dealings in the transfer market. But while his failure to sign Eric Cantona when he had the chance at Liverpool, and his cash happy attitude that saw several very average players brought to the club was a big part in the downfall of the Merseyside club, you would have to say that maybe, just maybe, he is not totally to blame.

After Kenny Dalglish took over as Liverpool manager in 1985 he achieved instant success winning the League and FA Cup double in his first season in charge. This was followed by more League titles in 1988 and 1990 and another FA cup win in 1989. It was looking like the little Scotsman was going to go down as one of the greatest managers in the history of the game. That was until he made the mind boggling signings of Jimmy Carter and David Speedie before quitting as Liverpool boss on 22nd February 1991. But by far his greatest mistake has to be that of signing Israeli international Ronny Rosenthal instead of German Legend Rudi Voller.

It was 1990 and Liverpool were looking for someone to partner Ian Rush after John Aldridge left to play for Real Sociedad in Spain the year before, and apparently Dalglish wanted Voller.

Voller had made his professional debut as a 17 year old, playing for Kickers Offenbach in the lower leagues of German football. But his deadly eye in front of goal was soon causing a stir among the bigger clubs, and in 1980, 1860 Munich, took the chance and gave the cheesy porn star look-alike his big break. During his two years in Munich, Voller, played 70 league games scoring an amazing 46 goals, earning himself a call up to the German Sqaud and a move to Werder Bremen. But it was while he was playing in Italy with AS Roma that Kenny Dalglish and Liverpool made their move. It was already half way through the 1989-1990 season and Roma were reluctant to let their star forward move away, but after Liverpool increased their initial bid and Voller stated his intentions to leave, the Italian side caved in and agreed to sell the German at the end of the season. While Liverpool were delighted with the deal, they were still short of a forward for the rest of the season. During a reserve team match against Luton Town the Liverpool backroom staff spotted Ronnie Rosenthal who was on trial at the London club from Udinese, and thought he could be the perfect stop gap until the Voller move was completed. Kenny Dalglish agreed, and on 22nd March 1990 Rosenthal joined Liverpool on loan until the end of the season. In his first full game Rosenthal scored a hat-trick against Charlton Athletic and followed that up with seven goals in the final eight games to secure Liverpool their record 18th league title. Liverpool instantly stumped 1.1 million GBP to make the move permanent, the highest fee ever paid by an English club for a foreign player. But the move also meant that they no longer had the money to bring Voller to England and he remained in Italy.

Liverpool would go on to regret their signing of Rosenthal instead of Voller as the Israeli international failed to make any sort of impact over the next 3 years. In 1992 he even went on to record the worst miss in the history of football when he hit the bar against Aston Villa from just eight yards out and with the goal keeper stranded on the edge of the box. Nice one Ronnie.

What If?

GERMAN STRIKER RUDI VOLLER SIGNED FOR LIVERPOOL on 8th July, 1990, two months after the Merseyside club had clinched their record eighteenth league title. It also spelled the end of a long search to a player to partner Ian Rush in attack that had also seen Israeli international Ronnie Rosenthal join the club on loan.

The Liverpool fans were excited by the new arrival, and the must have for every Kopite quickly became a blonde curly wig to match the hair style of their new hero. He made his debut on the opening day of the 1990-91 season against Sheffield Utd. Although Liverpool won the game easily 3-1, Voller struggled to make an impact and was substituted after just 65 minutes. Despite his first goal coming just three days later against Nottingham Forest, Voller continued to find it hard to adjust to the fast pace of English football and soon found himself warming the bench. By Christmas the talk was that Voller would soon be returning to Germany with Bayern Munich, but little did anyone know that he was about to be catapulted into the realm of Liverpool legend.

It was a fifth round FA Cup match between Liverpool and Everton that became one of the greatest Merseyside Derbies of all time. Liverpool took the lead three times, twice through Peter Beardsley and once through the scourge of every Evertonian, Ian Rush, only for Graeme Sharp and Tony Cottee to level the scores and take the game into extra time. After just seven minutes Liverpool scored a fourth through a spectacular right foot effort from winger John

Barnes. Many people thought it was a fluke, an attempted cross that ended up finding the far corner of the net. But the man himself says that while there was some luck involved, he was definitely going for goal.

"We were into extra time, and as I cut in from the left, I looked up and thought, 'Just try to hit the target.' It was my right foot but it still went curling past Neville Southall and into the far top corner," said Barnes, remembering the moment in an interview with *The Mail Online.* "Some people have suggested it was a cross, but it wasn't. No one can be 30 yards out and say, 'Right, I am going to put this on in that little space between the bar and post.' That would be ridiculous, but I was aiming in that direction. Normally you would expect a goal like that in extra time to be the killer blow, but we couldn't be sure. The way Everton kept coming back at us, there was always a nagging worry that they might come back at us."

And they did. With just six minutes remaining, Tony Cottee made it 4-4. Liverpool boss, Kenny Dalglish, realized that they had nothing left to lose and threw on Rudi Voller in a last gasp attempt to kill off his Merseyside rivals. It was a move inspired by God, as Voller lashed the ball in to Neville Southall's bottom right hand corner from 35 yards out with his first touch.

"I just closed my eyes and hit it," said Voller in a post match interview. But the German wasn't finished there, and as Everton pushed on again in an attempt to find a fifth equalizer, John Barnes played a long ball out of defence. Voller beat the offside trap, went one and one Southall and deftly chipped the ball over the oncoming keeper to seal an amazing 6-4 Liverpool win.

The game had a profound effect on Liverpool manager, Kenny Dalglish, who later admitted that the stress had nearly made him quit.

"When it got to 4-4 all I wanted to do was curl up into a

ball and be taken to some far away island. Instead I turned to Rudi and said, "Please get me out of this one." And Rudi saved my Liverpool career, there is no doubt about it."

The two goals not only saved Dalglish's Liverpool career, but also gave the German a new found confidence that he took into the final half of the season, scoring 11 goals to help Liverpool clinch their 19th League title. Voller was now a firm fans' favourite and over the next five seasons he scored an unbelievable 122 goals to cement his spot as a legend of the game.

Gambling Away a Career

From a very early age it was obvious that Paul Charles Merson was blessed with sublime talent. As an out and out left winger he was skilful and quick, and had an astute eye for goal. He was only 16 when he was picked up by Arsenal as an apprentice, and only 19 when he made his debut in the first team on 22nd November 1986 against Manchester City. His career at Arsenal was full of successes, 2 league titles in 1989 and 1991 as well as an FA Cup victory in 1993 and European Cup Winners cup success in 1994. All in all, Merson scored 99 goals for Arsenal before Arsene Wenger sold him on to Middlesbrough for 5 million GBP in 1997.

The move came as a bit of a surprise to the football world as Middlesbrough had just been relegated, and Merson at 29 was just reaching the peak of his prowess. But rather than setting him back, the move actually gave Merson's career a shot in the arm and saw him shake off some the stigma that was now attached to his name. He was selected for the 1998 England World Cup Squad in France and was the only member not at a top flight club. But his stay with Middlesbrough, up in the icy cold of the North East was only short, and after one season he decided to move on, but not before he had helped them achieve promotion back to the Premier League.

From here Merson moved to Aston Villa where he played more than a hundred games, and then in 2002 he joined Harry Redknapp at Portsmouth, where his outstanding displays helped another club achieve the dream of top flight English football. After a short spell as Manager of Walsall and playing just one game for non-league Tamworth, Paul Merson finally hung up his boots and packed away his shin pads ending a career that had seen him earn 21 England caps and win numerous trophies. But despite the successes that have followed Paul Merson to almost every club he has played for, he will always be remembered for the 1994 confession of his on-going battle with drink, drugs and gambling addictions.

Merson broke down in tears at a press conference as he let the world know about the demons that plagued his everyday life. The move seemed to split the many, so called, experts of the game in two. There were those who praised Merson for possessing the strength to come forward and admit his problems, while others thought that he should be instantly sacked and prosecuted for admitting to using cocaine. It was thought that making an example of Paul Merson would help prevent other young players from travelling down the same path. But despite all of his amazing admissions, Arsenal stuck by their man sending him to counselling sessions, and by the end of the 1994-95 season he was once again an integral part of the Arsenal set up.

Rumors of Merson's transgressions had apparently been floating around the back corridors of football for a long time. But they seemed to have remained just that, rumours, and it was only those at Arsenal that knew for certain what he was up to and they apparently wanted him out. What they needed was a patsy, someone who could be desperate enough to take on an alcoholic, cocaine sniffing, gambler; someone so desperate to keep their job that they would be willing to take almost any sort of risk. Enter Liverpool boss, Graeme Souness.

It was about one year before Merson's downward spiral was completed and he cried like a baby in front of the world's press. Souness and his Liverpool side were struggling and in need of something or someone that could give them a boost. Souness had already tried to buy his way out of trouble by splashing around large sums of money on the likes of Paul Stewart, Nigel Clough, Mark Wright and Dean Saunders, when he heard that Merson was having problems and could be available. Like a child who has just found out how to open the cookie jar and found it full to the brim of double chocolate chips, Souness dived in two-footed, tabling a 2 million GBP bid for the exciting but troubled winger. Arsenal instantly accepted, hoping that they had finally palmed Merson off before his bad habits hit the headlines. But the deal fell through when Graeme Souness was sacked following an embarrassing third round FA Cup defeat against Bristol City.

While on the surface it looked like Liverpool and Souness had got away with making another horrible transfer gaff, you only have to look at what Merson went on to achieve at other clubs to see that a move to Liverpool could have benefited both parties.

What If?

PAUL MERSON MADE HIS SURPRISE 2 MILLION GBP move from Arsenal to Liverpool on 1st December 1993 and made his debut just three days later as a substitute against Sheffield Wednesday. But it seemed that Merson was having trouble settling in at Anfield as he struggled to adapt to the new manager and his philosophies, showing nothing of the abilities that Souness had signed him for over his first few games. And after Liverpool suffered a humiliating 3-1 defeat away to Ipswich Town on 1st January 1994, with Merson being picked on by the press for another less than impressive display, the pressure was on both him and Souness to quickly to turn things around.

As Liverpool lined up to take on Bristol City in the third round of the FA Cup, the tension was high around Anfield as all the talk was about Souness and how his failure to win this match would be the final nail in his coffin.

The game kicked off in a silent almost eerie atmosphere at Anfield. It was as if the Liverpool fans were waiting eagerly and patiently to finally see the axe drop and the head of Graeme Souness roll. But when Liverpool took the lead after just ten minutes the atmosphere shifted. The Kop started singing and Liverpool were on a roll. Just fifteen minutes later, Merson picked up the ball wide on the left, drove past a City defender to the byline and pulled the ball back for Ian Rush to slot it in to the back of the net. It was Merson and Liverpool at their best, but could it continue?

Liverpool won the game 5-1, with Paul Merson bagging two and picking up the Man of the Match award. It was a great performance by the reds, but the football press couldn't help but point out that it was only against Bristol City as they kept the pressure up on Souness. But the win had subdued the panic that was beginning to build in the board room and the noose around his neck was loosened ever so slightly. The rest of the season continued in the same vein. Liverpool and Merson in particular, were on fire. They lost just twice on a run that saw them finish a respectable fifth in the league. On their final game of the season against Aston Villa, the Liverpool steam train was in full effect. Merson was tormenting the Villa defence all day, and Robbie Fowler looked sharp up front. Liverpool finished their season on a high winning 3-0, and all the talk was of a possible title challenge for next season.

After the match at Villa Park, Graeme Souness invited his players to his house for an end of season bash. The party was intended to be a bonding session, food, a few drinks and deep discussion of which players could be added to the squad for the next season to move them forward. But the players had a different idea, and after many beers and a few bottles of Scotch, a full blown party had broken out. Souness decided to leave the lads to it and let them blow off some steam. They could talk tactics when they all returned to pre-season training.

"I went to bed at around 2am," said Souness in a 2003 interview with Britain's *Daily Mail* newspaper, "leaving some of the players down stairs drinking. When I opened my bedroom door I couldn't believe my eyes. There was Merse (Paul Merson) snorting cocaine off my bed-side table. He nearly had a heart attack when I clipped him around the ear. He begged me to forgive him, to give him another chance. He had been our best player all season so I did. I made him promise that he would clean himself up before pre-season, then I closed the door and let him get on with it."

Souness had total faith in his player, total faith that his understanding approach would work and Merson would hibernate for four weeks and come back stronger for the new season. How wrong he was. Far from going in to rehab, Merson thought that his boss had simply turned a blind eye to his habit and given him permission to continue. The day after the end of season party, Merson and a few of the boys flew to Las Vegas to continue the blow out, with the understanding that what happened in Vegas would be well and truly suffocated and buried in a shallow grave deep in the Nevada desert. But, unfortunately for them, they had shared the same plane as a freelance journalist who instantly spotted a story.

"The players were drinking and being so loud," said journalist Andrew Blower, "I thought this on its own would have been a great story, but I decided to follow them to Vegas just to see what happened next." The decision would make his career.

On the first night, Merson and his friends went straight to the MGM Grand casino. Martin couldn't believe his eyes as Paul Merson gambled away thousands and thousands of dollars, flirted with anything in a skirt and drank giant cocktails like a fish.

Andrew Blower was shocked. "I couldn't believe my eyes. Here was one of England's top footballers, a superstar, a role model with very obvious problems." But it was the photographs that he would pick up at a party in the player's hotel room later in the week that would shock the world. "I managed to get invited to his room for a party, and he was openly snorting cocaine off the table, totally out of his mind. It was a very sad sight."

Far from showing Merson any sympathy Andrew Blower sold his story to the highest bidder, Britain's *Sun* newspaper. The pictures rocked the football world and especially the Liverpool Football Club. The board of directors forced Merson to call a press conference to explain the extent of his addictions. The player broke down as he talked about the drink, drugs and gambling addictions that were threatening to destroy his life. The press jumped on it and insisted he be sacked from the club, but Liverpool decided to stand by their troubled star and promised to give him the best help possible so that he could defeat his demons. Instead, it was Graeme Sounes who paid the ultimate price. In a statement released to the press following the sacking of Souness, the Liverpool Chairman said, "It has come to light that Graeme Souness was well aware of the problems surrounding Paul Merson and said nothing in order to save his own skin. This is a club run on honesty and integrity and anyone who fails to show those has no place here."

But everyone in the game knew it was an easy way to get rid of the man they had wanted to sack for the past nine months.

Paul Merson took his place in the Liverpool starting line up for the opening day of the 1994-95 season against Crystal Palace despite still undergoing intensive rehabilitation. New boss, Roy Evans, saw that keeping the England international involved in first team football was an integral part of his recovery. Paul Merson repaid this massive faith in him by helping guide Liverpool to a third place Premier League finish as well as a League Cup win. Merson went on to become a Liverpool legend playing more than 200 times and winning the League title in 1997, before being sold to Aston Villa for 2 million GBP in 1998.

IT could have all happened, HONEST.

Lightning Source UK Ltd.
Milton Keynes UK

171793UK00001B/3/P